ACCLAIM FOR ...ER:

"Explosive, thrilling, action-packed – meet Alex Rider." **Guardian**

"Horowitz is pure class, stylish but action-packed ... being James Bond in miniature is way cooler than being a wizard." **Daily Mirror**

"Horowitz will grip you with suspense, daring and cheek – and that's just the first page! ... Prepare for action scenes as fast as a movie." **The Times**

"Anthony Horowitz is the lion of children's literature." **Michael Morpurgo**

"Fast and furious." **Telegraph**

"The perfect hero ... genuine 21st century stuff." **Daily Telegraph**

"Brings new meaning to the phrase 'action-packed'." **Sunday Times**

"Every bored schoolboy's fantasy, only a thousand times funnier, slicker and more exciting ... genius." **Independent on Sunday**

"Perfect escapism for all teenage boys."
The Times

"Addictive, pacey novels."   *Financial Times*

"Adults as well as kids will be hooked on the
adventures of Alex Rider ... Harry Potter with
attitude."   *Daily Express*

"Meaty, thrilling and compelling."
Irish Independent

"This is the kind of book that's designed to grab
the reader by the scruff of the neck, pull him
into the page and not let go of him until he's
well and truly hooked."   *The Good Book Guide*

"If you are looking for a thrilling, exciting read,
this is it."   *Sunday Express*

"Crackling with suspense and daring, this is a
fabulous story, showing that a bit of guts will
take you a very long way."   *Guardian*

"Will last for ever as one of the children's
classics of our age."   *The Times*

"The series that has re-invented the spy genre."
Independent

Titles by Anthony Horowitz

The Alex Rider series:
Stormbreaker
Point Blanc
Skeleton Key
Eagle Strike
Scorpia
Ark Angel
Snakehead
Crocodile Tears
Scorpia Rising
Russian Roulette
Never Say Die
Secret Weapon

The Power of Five (Book One): *Raven's Gate*
The Power of Five (Book Two): *Evil Star*
The Power of Five (Book Three): *Nightrise*
The Power of Five (Book Four): *Necropolis*
The Power of Five (Book Five): *Oblivion*

The Devil and his Boy
Granny
Groosham Grange
Return to Groosham Grange
The Switch
Scared to Death

The Diamond Brothers books:
The Falcon's Malteser
Public Enemy Number Two
South by South East
The French Confection
The Greek Who Stole Christmas
The Blurred Man
I Know What You Did Last Wednesday

ALEX RIDER

ACTION
ADRENALINE
ADVENTURE

STORMBREAKER

ANTHONY HOROWITZ

WALKER
BOOKS

For J, N, C and L

First published 2000 by Walker Books Ltd
87 Vauxhall Walk, London SE11 5HJ

This edition published 2020

2 4 6 8 10 9 7 5 3 1

Text © 2000 Stormbreaker Productions Ltd
Introduction and extract © 2020 Stormbreaker Productions Ltd
Cover illustration © 2015 Walker Books Ltd
Trademarks Alex Rider™; Boy with Torch Logo™
© 2010 Stormbreaker Productions Ltd

The right of Anthony Horowitz to be identified as author
of this work has been asserted by him in accordance with
the Copyright, Designs and Patents Act 1988

This book has been typeset in Officina Sans

Printed and bound by CPI Group (UK) Ltd, Croydon CR0 4YY

British Library Cataloguing in Publication Data:
a catalogue record for this book
is available from the British Library

ISBN 978-1-4063-8858-9

www.walker.co.uk
www.walkerbooks.com.au

MIX
Paper from
responsible sources
FSC® C020471
FSC
www.fsc.org

CONTENTS

TWENTY YEARS OF ALEX

It's almost impossible to believe that it was twenty years ago that I wrote *Stormbreaker* but I still remember exactly the moment that Alex Rider was born.

I was living in Crouch End, north London. I had a lovely house with a little studio at the bottom of the garden, a white bunkhouse that was partly submerged below the ground with views across the lawn. It was my private space – there was even a bedroom which I used if I worked late into the night.

By then, I had written ten books for children, including *Granny*, *Groosham Grange, The Diamond Brothers*, *The Devil and his Boy* and *The Switch*. Writing for children had become a passion of mine, although I'm not quite sure why. Maybe it was because my own childhood had been so peculiar – slightly Victorian with nannies and gardeners, odd parents and five years at an unpleasant prep school. I loved writing stories about adventure and escape. I loved the fast pace and the uncomplicated narrative that children's books offered. I was still sure that there was a larger audience out there. The only question was – how could I reach it?

That was when I remembered an idea I'd had a long time before.

Growing up, I had always loved the James Bond movies. They were the one event in the year that I looked forward to. Of course, Sean Connery was my favourite Bond (I was eight years old when the first film, *Dr No*, came out) but I liked Roger Moore too. The trouble was that Moore played the part for so long that by the end he had got rather old. He was actually fifty-seven when he played Bond for the last time in *A View to a Kill* and, watching that film, I'd had a sudden thought. Wouldn't it be great if Bond was a teenager! Why not write the story of a boy who becomes a spy?

Although I didn't know it at the time, this was the light-bulb moment that would change my life.

Cut forward now to 1999 and I'm sitting in my studio, thinking about that idea. I reach for my notepad and, with a fountain pen – which is what I always use for my first drafts – I write the following sentence:

"When the doorbell rings at three in the morning, it's never good news."

Looking at what I'd just written, I knew that I had stumbled onto something different.

What was it?

Well, first of all, the sentence doesn't sound like the opening of a children's book. It's quite dark. It's intriguing. It opens a door into a new world and invites you in.

It's also quite adult. Even before I had fully worked out the plot of *Stormbreaker*, I had decided that it wouldn't be a children's book at all. It would be an adult book for kids. Unlike the heroes I had created, Alex wouldn't act as if he was in a children's book. He would be a real teenager. My earlier stories had been full of references to my own childhood – peculiar parents, unpleasant schools. But Alex would be as unlike me as I could make him. I went to a private school. He would go to a comprehensive. I liked books and reading. He would like sport. Above all, he would be a reluctant hero. That was the most important thing for me. Alex wouldn't always enjoy his adventures. He would get hurt. His life wouldn't be easy.

Where did the character of Alex come from? Well, there is a little bit of Bond in there. A lot of him was inspired by my son, Nicholas, who was ten years old at the time, very athletic and completely fearless. Another boy also came for lunch while I was working on the idea, the son of my two closest friends. He spoke two languages and he was learning a martial art and he even looked a bit like a young spy. His name was Alex ... which struck me at once as perfect. Nice and short and ending in X. I thought a lot before I settled on Rider. I wanted an old-fashioned English name, something short and easy to spell. I thought of knights who used to ride on horses. One of my favourite adventure writers was a man called H. Rider Haggard. And going back to *Dr No*, the love interest in that film was Honeychile Ryder.

The choice was made.

Although I had been inspired by Bond, I did everything I could to make Alex as different as possible. First of all, he doesn't want to be a spy. While Bond has a close relationship with his boss, Alex doesn't like MI6 very much at all. Originally, there were going to be no gadgets in the Alex Rider books. Gadgets, of course, have always been a huge feature of the James Bond films and that was a good reason not to have them. But I changed my mind after talking about the idea in twenty or thirty schools. "What gadgets are you going to have?" That was the question I was asked over and over again and I realized that young readers would be disappointed if there weren't any at all. Even so, I made my gadget master, Smithers, as different as I could from Q in the films (although Smithers is actually the name of a minor character in the James Bond book, *Goldfinger*).

All the plots for the Alex Rider books have been inspired by stories I have read in the newspapers and the first novel was no different.

Stormbreaker was inspired by an Egyptian businessman who had appeared in many newspaper stories. I was fascinated by the fact that although he was a billionaire, employed lots of people and seemed to love living in England, everyone was always writing horrible things about him. He was a complete outsider. At the same time, I read about a computer virus that was spreading across the world – it was called the Melissa virus and it caused about one hundred million pounds worth of damage. I put the two together and came up with an idea about a billionaire working in the computer industry who takes revenge on the English for treating him so badly – and that is the book you have in your hands. Incidentally, the original title was *Stormchaser*. I had to change it when another book with exactly the same title suddenly appeared.

So here I am twenty years later and sometimes it seems unfair to me that I'm so much older while Alex has only aged fifteen months. I have now written thirteen novels including one collection of short stories – *Secret Weapon*. My publishers tell me that the books have sold millions of copies worldwide but to be honest that doesn't make much difference to me. I still spend most of my life sitting in a room on my own – which is where I am writing this.

So much has happened since the publication of *Stormbreaker*. It was turned into a film, of course, and now *Point Blanc* has been turned into a television series with a wonderful actor, Otto Farrant, playing Alex. The thirteenth Alex Rider novel, *Nightshade*, is about to be published and there will be at least one more after that.

Right now, there's a whole new generation of readers who are discovering Alex and it's great to think that my stories have been a part of their lives and have helped them to discover the pleasure of reading.

That's the end of the introduction, specially written for this twentieth anniversary edition.

I wonder if anyone has read it? If it had been me, I certainly wouldn't have bothered. I'd have just dived straight into the story. At the end of the day, Alex Rider speaks for himself.

Anthony Horowitz

FUNERAL VOICES

When the doorbell rings at three in the morning, it's never good news.

Alex Rider was woken by the first chime. His eyes flickered open but for a moment he stayed completely still in his bed, lying on his back with his head resting on the pillow. He heard a bedroom door open and a creak of wood as somebody went downstairs. The bell rang a second time and he looked at the alarm clock glowing beside him. 3.02 a.m. There was a rattle as someone slid the security chain off the front door.

He rolled out of bed and walked over to the open window, his bare feet pressing down the carpet pile. The moonlight spilled on to his chest and shoulders. Alex was fourteen, already well-built, with the body of an athlete. His hair, cut short apart from two thick strands hanging over his forehead, was fair. His eyes were brown and serious. For a moment he stood silently, half-hidden in the shadow, looking out. There was a police car parked outside. From his second-floor window Alex could see the black ID number on the roof and the caps of the two men who were standing in front of the door. The porch light went on and, at the same time, the door opened.

"Mrs Rider?"

"No. I'm the housekeeper. What is it? What's happened?"

"This is the home of Mr Ian Rider?"

"Yes."

"I wonder if we could come in..."

And Alex already knew. He knew from the way the police stood there, awkward and unhappy. But he also knew from the tone of their voices. Funeral voices ... that was how he would describe them later. The sort of voices people use when they come to tell you that someone close to you has died.

He went to his door and opened it. He could hear the two policemen talking down in the hall, but only some of the words reached him.

"...a car accident ... called the ambulance ... intensive care ... nothing anyone could do ... so sorry."

It was only hours later, sitting in the kitchen, watching as the grey light of morning bled slowly through the west London streets, that Alex could try to make sense of what had happened. His uncle – Ian Rider – was dead. Driving home, his car had been hit by a lorry at Old Street roundabout and he had been killed almost instantly. He hadn't been wearing a seat-belt, the police said. Otherwise, he might have had a chance.

Alex thought of the man who had been his only relation for as long as he could remember. He had never known his own parents. They had died in an accident, that one a plane crash, a few weeks after he had been born. He had been brought up by his father's brother (never "uncle" – Ian Rider had hated that word) and had spent most of his fourteen years in the same terraced house in Chelsea, London, between the King's Road and the river. But it was only now Alex realized just how little he knew about the man.

A banker. People said Alex looked quite like him. Ian Rider was always travelling. A quiet, private man who liked good wine, classical music and books. Who didn't seem to have any girl-friends … in fact he didn't have any friends at all. He had kept himself fit, had never smoked and had dressed expensively. But that wasn't enough. That wasn't a picture of a life. It was only a thumbnail sketch.

"Are you all right, Alex?" A young woman had come into the room. She was in her late twenties, with a sprawl of red hair and a round, boyish face. Jack Starbright was American. She had come to London as a student seven years ago, rented a room in the house – in return for light housework and baby-sitting duties – and had stayed on to become housekeeper and one of Alex's closest friends. Sometimes he wondered what the Jack was short for. Jackie? Jacqueline? Neither of them suited her and although he had once asked, she had never said.

Alex nodded. "What do you think will happen?" he asked.

"What do you mean?"

"To the house. To me. To you."

"I don't know." She shrugged. "I guess Ian will have made a will. He'll have left instructions."

"Maybe we should look in his office."

"Yes. But not today, Alex. Let's take it one step at a time."

Ian's office was a room running the full length of the house, high up at the top. It was the only room that was always locked – Alex had only been in there three or four times, never on his own.

When he was younger, he had fantasized that there might be something strange up there; a time machine or a UFO. But it was only an office with a desk, a couple of filing cabinets, shelves full of papers and books. Bank stuff – that's what Ian said. Even so, Alex wanted to go up there now. Because it had never been allowed.

"The police said he wasn't wearing his seat-belt." Alex turned to look at Jack.

She nodded. "Yes. That's what they said."

"Doesn't that seem strange to you? You know how careful he was. He always wore his seat-belt. He wouldn't even drive me round the corner without making me put mine on."

Jack thought for a moment, then shrugged. "Yeah, it's strange," she said. "But that must have been the way it was. Why would the police have lied?"

The day dragged on. Alex hadn't gone to school even though, secretly, he had wanted to. He would have preferred to escape back into normal life – the clang of the bell, the crowds of familiar faces – instead of sitting there, trapped inside the house. But he had to be there for the visitors who came throughout the morning and the rest of the afternoon.

There were five of them. A solicitor who knew nothing about a will, but seemed to have been charged with organizing the funeral. A funeral director who had been recommended by the solicitor. A vicar – tall, elderly – who seemed disappointed that Alex didn't look more upset. A neighbour from across the road – how did she even know that anyone had died? And finally a man from the bank.

"All of us at the Royal & General are deeply shocked," he said. He was in his thirties, wearing a polyester suit with a Marks & Spencer tie. He had the sort of face you forgot even while you were looking at it, and had introduced himself as Crawley, from Personnel. "But if there's anything we can do..."

"What will happen?" Alex asked for the second time that day.

"You don't have to worry," Crawley said. "The bank will take care of everything. That's my job. You leave everything to me."

The day passed. Alex killed a couple of hours in the evening playing his Playstation – and then felt vaguely guilty when Jack caught him at it. But what else was he to do? Later on she took him to a Burger King. He was glad to get out of the house, but the two of them barely spoke. Alex assumed Jack would have to go back to America. She certainly couldn't stay in London for ever. So who would look after him? By law, he was still too young to look after himself. His whole future looked so uncertain that he preferred not to talk about it. He preferred not to talk at all.

And then the day of the funeral arrived and Alex found himself dressed in a dark jacket, preparing to leave in a black car that had come from nowhere, surrounded by people he had never met. Ian Rider was buried in the Brompton Cemetery on the Fulham Road, just in the shadow of Chelsea football ground, and Alex knew where he would have preferred to be on that Wednesday afternoon. About thirty people had turned up but he hardly recognized any of them. A grave had been dug close to the lane that ran the length of the cemetery and as the service began, a black Rolls-Royce drew up, the back door opened and a man got out. Alex watched him as he walked forward and stopped. Overhead, a plane coming in to land at Heathrow momentarily blotted out the sun. Alex shivered. There was something about the new arrival that made his skin crawl.

And yet the man was ordinary to look at. Grey suit, grey hair, grey lips and grey eyes. His face was expressionless, the eyes behind the square, gunmetal spectacles completely empty. Perhaps that was what disturbed Alex. Whoever this man was, he seemed to have less life than anyone in the cemetery. Above or below ground.

Someone tapped Alex on the shoulder and he turned round to see Mr Crawley leaning over him. "That's Mr Blunt," the personnel manager whispered. "He's the chairman of the bank."

Alex's eyes travelled past Blunt and over to the Rolls-Royce. Two more men had come with him, one of them the driver. They were wearing identical suits and, although it wasn't a particularly bright day, sunglasses. Both of them were watching the funeral with the same grim faces. Alex looked from them to Blunt and then to the other people who had come to the cemetery. Had they really known Ian Rider? Why had he never met any of them before? And why did he find it so difficult to believe that any of them really worked for a bank?

"...a good man, a patriotic man. He will be missed."

The vicar had finished his grave-side address. His choice of words struck Alex as odd. Patriotic? That meant he loved his country. But as far as Alex knew, Ian Rider had barely spent any time in it. Certainly he had never been one for waving the Union Jack. He looked round, hoping to find Jack, but saw instead that Blunt was making his way towards him, stepping carefully round the grave.

"You must be Alex." The chairman was only a little taller than him. Close to, his skin was strangely unreal. It could have been made of plastic. "My name is Alan Blunt," he said. "Your uncle often spoke about you."

"That's funny," Alex said. "He never mentioned you."

The grey lips twitched briefly. "We'll miss him. He was a good man."

"What was he good at?" Alex asked. "He never talked about his work."

Suddenly Crawley was there. "Your uncle was Overseas Finance Manager, Alex," he said. "He was responsible for our foreign branches. You must have known that."

"I know he travelled a lot," Alex said. "And I know he was very careful. About things like seat-belts."

"Well, sadly he wasn't careful enough." Blunt's eyes, magnified by the thick lenses of his spectacles, lasered into his own and for a moment Alex felt himself pinned down, like an insect under a microscope. "I hope we'll meet again,"

Blunt went on. He tapped the side of his face with a single grey finger. "Yes..." Then he turned and went back to his car.

It was as he was getting into the Rolls-Royce that it happened. The driver leaned across to open the back door and his jacket fell open, revealing the shirt underneath. And not just the shirt. The man was wearing a leather holster with an automatic pistol strapped inside. Alex saw it even as the man, realizing what had happened, quickly straightened up and pulled the jacket across his chest. Blunt had seen it too. He turned back and looked again at Alex. Something very close to an emotion slithered over his face. Then he got into the car, the door closed and he was gone.

A gun at a funeral. Why? Why would bank managers carry guns?

"Let's get out of here." Suddenly Jack was at his side. "Cemeteries give me the creeps."

"Yes. And quite a few creeps have turned up," Alex muttered.

They slipped away quietly and went home. The car that had taken them to the funeral was still waiting, but they preferred the open air. The walk took them fifteen minutes. As they turned the corner into their street, Alex noticed a removals van parked in front of the house, the words

STRYKER & SON painted on its side.

"What's that doing...?" he began.

At the same moment, the van shot off, its wheels skidding over the surface of the road.

Alex said nothing as Jack unlocked the door and let them in, but while she went into the kitchen to make some tea, he looked quickly round the house. A letter that had been on the hall table now lay on the carpet. A door that had been half-open was now closed. Tiny details, but Alex's eyes missed nothing. Somebody had been in the house. He was almost sure of it.

But he wasn't certain until he got to the top floor. The door to the office which had always, always been locked, was unlocked now. Alex opened it and went in. The room was empty. Ian Rider had gone and so had everything else. The desk drawers, the cupboards, the shelves ... anything that might have told him about the dead man's work had been taken.

"Alex...!" Jack was calling to him from downstairs.

Alex took one last look around the forbidden room, wondering again about the man who had once worked there. Then he closed the door and went back down.

HEAVEN FOR CARS

With Hammersmith Bridge just ahead of him, Alex left the river and swung his bike through the lights and down the hill towards Brookland School. The bike was a Condor Junior Roadracer, custom-built for him on his twelfth birthday. It was a teenager's bike with a cut-down Reynolds 531 frame, but the wheels were full-sized so he could ride at speed with hardly any rolling resistance. He spun past a Mini and cut through the school gates. He would be sorry when he grew out of the bike. For two years now it had almost been part of him.

He double-locked it in the shed and went into the yard. Brookland was a new comprehensive, red brick and glass, modern and ugly. Alex could have gone to any of the smart private schools around Chelsea, but Ian Rider had decided to send him here. He had said it would be more of a challenge.

The first lesson of the day was maths. When Alex came into the classroom, the teacher, Mr Donovan, was already scribbling on the whiteboard, setting out a complicated equation. It was hot in the room, the sunlight streaming in through the floor-to-ceiling windows put in by architects who should have known better. As Alex took his place near the back, he wondered how he was going to get through the lesson. How could he possibly think about algebra when there were so many other questions churning through his mind?

The gun at the funeral. The way Blunt had looked at him. The van with STRYKER & SON written on the side. The empty office. And the biggest question of all, the one detail that refused to go away. The seat-belt. Ian Rider hadn't been wearing a seat-belt.

But of course he had.

Ian Rider had never been one to give lectures. He had always said Alex should make up his own mind about things. But he'd had this thing about seat-belts. The more Alex thought about it, the less he believed it. A collision at a roundabout. Suddenly he wished he could see the car. At least

29

the wreckage would tell him that the accident had really happened, that Ian Rider really had died that way.

"Alex?"

Alex looked up and realized that everyone was staring at him. Mr Donovan had just asked him something. He quickly scanned the whiteboard, taking in the figures. "Yes, sir," he said, "x equals seven and y is fifteen."

The maths teacher sighed. "Yes, Alex. You're absolutely right. But actually I was just asking you to open the window."

Somehow he managed to get through the rest of the day, but by the time the final bell rang, his mind was made up. While everyone else streamed out, he made his way to the secretary's office and borrowed a local directory.

"What are you looking for?" the secretary asked. Jane Bedfordshire was a young woman in her twenties, and she'd always had a soft spot for Alex.

"Breakers' yards..." Alex flicked through the pages. "If a car got smashed up near Old Street, they'd take it somewhere near by, wouldn't they?"

"I suppose so."

"Here..." Alex had found the yards listed under

"Car Dismantlers". But there were dozens of them fighting for attention over four pages.

"Is this for a school project?" the secretary asked. She knew Alex had lost a relative, but not how.

"Sort of..." Alex was reading the addresses, but they told him nothing.

"This one's quite near Old Street." Miss Bedfordshire pointed at the corner of the page.

"Wait!" Alex tugged the book towards him and looked at the entry underneath the one the secretary had chosen:

J.B. STRYKER
Heaven for cars...
J.B. Stryker, Auto Breakers
Lambeth Walk, LONDON
Tel: 020 7123 5392
...call us today!

"That's in Vauxhall," Miss Bedfordshire said. "Not too far from here."

"I know." But Alex had recognized the name. J.B. Stryker. He thought back to the van he had seen outside his house on the day of the funeral. STRYKER & SON. Of course it might just be a coincidence, but it was still somewhere to start. He closed the book. "I'll see you, Miss Bedfordshire."

"Be careful how you go." The secretary watched

Alex leave, wondering why she had said that. Maybe it was his eyes. Dark and serious, there was something dangerous there. Then the phone rang and she forgot him as she went back to work.

J.B. Stryker's was a square of wasteland behind the railway tracks running out of Waterloo Station. The area was enclosed by a high brick wall topped with broken glass and razor wire. Two wooden gates hung open, and from the other side of the road Alex could see a shed with a security window and beyond it the tottering piles of dead and broken cars. Everything of any value had been stripped away and only the rusting carcasses remained, heaped one on top of the other, waiting to be fed into the crusher.

There was a guard sitting in the shed, reading the *Sun*. In the distance, a crane coughed into life, then roared down on a battered Ford Mondeo, its metal claw smashing through the window to scoop up the vehicle and carry it away. A phone rang somewhere in the shed and the guard turned round to answer it. That was enough for Alex. Holding his bike and wheeling it along beside him, he sprinted through the gates.

He found himself surrounded by dirt and

debris. The smell of diesel was thick in the air and the roar of the engines was deafening. Alex watched as the crane swooped down on another of the cars, seized it in a metallic grip and dropped it into a crusher. For a moment the car rested on a pair of shelves. Then the shelves lifted up, toppling the car over and down into a trough. The operator – sitting in a glass cabin at one end of the crusher – pressed a button and there was a great belch of black smoke. The shelves closed in on the car like a monster insect folding in its wings. There was a grinding sound as the car was crushed until it was no bigger than a rolled-up carpet. Then the operator threw a gear and the car was squeezed out, metallic toothpaste being chopped up by a hidden blade. The slices tumbled on to the ground.

Leaving his bike propped against the wall, Alex ran further into the yard, crouching down behind the wrecks. With the din from the machines, there was no chance that anyone would hear him, but he was still afraid of being seen. He stopped to catch his breath, drawing a grimy hand across his face. His eyes were watering from the diesel fumes. The air was as filthy as the ground beneath him.

He was beginning to regret coming – but then

he saw it. His uncle's BMW was parked a few metres away, separated from the other cars. At first glance it looked absolutely fine, the metallic silver bodywork not even scratched. Certainly there was no way this car could have been involved in a fatal collision with a lorry or anything else. But it was his uncle's car. Alex recognized the number plate. He hurried closer, and it was then he saw that the car was damaged after all. The windscreen had been smashed, along with all the windows on one side. Alex made his way round the bonnet. He reached the other side. And froze.

Ian Rider hadn't died in any accident. What had killed him was plain to see – even to someone who had never seen such a thing before. A spray of bullets had caught the car full on the driver's side, shattering the front tyre, then smashing the windscreen and side windows and punching into the side panels. Alex ran his fingers over the holes. The metal felt cold against his flesh. He opened the door and looked inside. The front seats, pale grey leather, were strewn with fragments of broken glass and stained with patches of dark brown. He didn't need to ask what the stains were. He could see everything. The flash of the machine-gun, the bullets ripping into the car, Ian Rider jerking in the driver's seat...

But why? Why kill a bank manager? And why had the murder been covered up? It was the police who had brought the news, so they must be part of it. Had they deliberately lied? None of it made sense.

"You should have got rid of it two days ago. Do it now."

The machines must have stopped for a moment. If there hadn't been a sudden lull, Alex would never have heard the men coming. Quickly he looked across the steering-wheel and out the other side. There were two of them, both dressed in loose-fitting overalls. Alex had a feeling he'd seen them before. At the funeral. One of them was the driver, the man he had seen with the gun. He was sure of it.

Whoever they were, they were only a few paces away from the car, talking in low voices. Another few steps and they would be there. Without thinking, Alex threw himself into the only hiding place available, inside the car itself. Using his foot, he hooked the door and closed it. At the same time, he became aware that the machines had started again and he could no longer hear the men. He didn't dare look up. A shadow fell across the window as the two men passed. But then they were gone. He was safe.

And then something hit the BMW with such force that Alex cried out, his whole body caught in a massive shock wave that tore him away from the steering-wheel and threw him helplessly into the back. At the same time, the roof buckled and three huge metal fingers tore through the skin of the car like a fork through an eggshell, trailing dust and sunlight. One of the fingers grazed the side of his head – any closer and it would have cracked his skull. Alex yelled as blood trickled over his eye. He tried to move, then was jerked back a second time as the car was yanked off the ground and tilted high up in the air.

He couldn't see. He couldn't move. But his stomach lurched as the car swung in an arc, the metal grinding and the light spinning. It had been picked up by the crane. It was going to be put inside the crusher. With him inside.

He tried to raise himself up, to punch through the windows. But the claw of the crane had already flattened the roof, pinning his left leg, perhaps even breaking it. He could feel nothing. He lifted a hand and managed to pound on the back window, but he couldn't break the glass, and even if the workmen were staring at the BMW, they would never see anything moving inside.

His short flight across the breaker's yard ended with a bone-shattering crash as the crane deposited the car on the iron shelves of the crusher. Alex tried to fight back his sickness and despair and think of what to do. He had seen a car being processed only a few minutes before. Any moment now, the operator would send the car tipping into the coffin-shaped trough. The machine was a Lefort Shear, a slow-motion guillotine. At the press of a button, the two wings would close on the car with a joint pressure of five hundred tonnes. The car, with Alex inside it, would be crushed beyond recognition. And the broken metal – and flesh – would then be chopped into sections. Nobody would ever know what had happened.

He tried with all his strength to free himself. But the roof was too low. His leg and part of his back were trapped. Then his whole world tilted and he felt himself falling into darkness. The shelves had lifted. The BMW slid to one side and fell the few metres into the trough. Alex felt the metalwork collapsing all around him. The back window exploded and glass showered around his head, dust and diesel fumes punching into his nose and eyes. There was hardly any daylight now, but looking out of the back he could see the huge steel head of the piston that would push what was left of the car through the exit hole on the other side.

The engine tone of the Lefort Shear changed as it prepared for the final act. The metal wings shuddered. In a few seconds' time, the two of them would meet, crumpling the BMW like a paper bag.

Alex pulled with all his strength and was astonished when his leg came free. It took him perhaps a second – one precious second – to work out what had happened. When the car had fallen into the trough, it had landed on its side. The roof had buckled again ... enough to free him. His hand scrabbled for the door – but of course that was useless. The doors were too bent. They would never open. The back window! With the glass gone, he could crawl through the frame, but only if he moved fast...

The wings began to move. The BMW screamed as two walls of solid steel relentlessly crushed it. Glass shattered. One of the wheel axles snapped with the sound of a thunderbolt. The darkness closed in. Alex grabbed hold of what was left of the back seat. Ahead of him he could see a single triangle of light, shrinking faster and faster. With all his strength, he surged forward, finding some sort of purchase on the gear column. He could feel the weight of the two walls pressing down on him. Behind him the car was no longer a car, but the fist of some hideous monster snatching at the insect that he had become.

His shoulders passed through the triangle, out into the light. But his legs were still inside. If his foot snagged on something he would be squeezed into two pieces. Alex yelled out loud and jerked his knee forward. His legs came clear, then his feet, but at the last moment his shoe caught on the closing triangle and disappeared back into the car. Alex imagined he heard the sound of the leather being squashed, but that was impossible. Clinging to the black, oily surface of the observation platform at the back of the crusher, he dragged himself clear and managed to stand up.

He found himself face to face with a man so fat that he could barely fit into the small cabin of the crusher. The man's stomach was pressed against the glass, his shoulders squeezed into the corners. A cigarette dangled on his lower lip as his mouth fell open and his eyes stared. In front of him was a boy in the rags of what had once been a school uniform. A whole sleeve had been torn off and his arm, streaked with blood and oil, hung limply by his side. By the time the operator had taken all this in, come to his senses and turned the machine off, Alex had gone.

He clambered down the side of the crusher, landing on the one foot that still had a shoe. He was aware now of pieces of jagged metal lying everywhere. If he wasn't careful, he would cut the other foot open. His bicycle was where he had left it, leaning against the wall, and gingerly, half-hopping, he made for it. Behind him he heard the cabin of the crusher open and a man's voice call out, raising the alarm. At the same time, a second man ran forward, stopping between Alex and his bike. It was the driver, the man he had seen at the funeral. His face, twisted into a hostile frown, was curiously ugly; greasy hair, watery eyes, pale, lifeless skin.

"What do you think...!" he began. His hand slid into his jacket. Alex remembered the gun and instantly, without even thinking, swung into action.

He had started learning karate when he was six years old. One afternoon, with no explanation, Ian Rider had taken him to a local club for his first lesson and he had been going there, once a week, ever since. Over the years he had passed through the various *Kyu* – student – grades. But it was only the year before that he had become a first grade *Dan*, a black belt. When he had arrived at Brookland School, his looks and accent had quickly brought him to the attention of the school bullies; three hulking sixteen-year-olds. They had cornered him once behind the bike shed. The encounter had lasted less than a minute, and after it one of the bullies had left Brookland and the other two had never troubled anyone again.

Now Alex brought up one leg, twisted his body round and lashed out. The back kick – *Ushiro-geri* – is said to be the most lethal in karate. His foot powered into the man's abdomen with such force that he didn't even have time to cry out. His eyes bulged and his mouth half-opened in surprise. Then, with his hand still halfway into his jacket, he crumpled to the ground.

Alex jumped over him, snatched up his bike and swung himself on to it. In the distance, a third man was running towards him. He heard the single word "Stop!" called out. Then there was a crack and a bullet whipped past. Alex gripped the handlebars and pedalled as hard as he could. The bike shot forward, over the rubble and out through the gates. He took one look over his shoulder. Nobody had followed him.

With one shoe on and one shoe off, his clothes

in rags and his body streaked with blood and oil, Alex knew he must look a strange sight. But then he thought back to his last seconds inside the crusher and sighed with relief. He could have been looking a lot worse.

ROYAL & GENERAL

The bank rang the following day.

"This is John Crawley. Do you remember me? Personnel Manager at the Royal & General. We were wondering if you could come in."

"Come in?" Alex was half-dressed, already late for school.

"This afternoon. We found some papers of your uncle's. We need to talk to you ... about your own position."

Was there something faintly threatening in the man's voice? "What time this afternoon?" Alex asked.

"Could you manage half-past four? We're on Liverpool Street. We can send a cab—"

"I'll be there," Alex said. "And I'll take the tube."

He hung up.

"Who was that?" Jack called out from the kitchen. She was cooking breakfast for the two of them, although how long she could remain with Alex was a growing worry. Her wages hadn't been paid. She had only her own money to buy food and pay for the running of the house. Worse still, her visa was about to expire. Soon she wouldn't even be allowed to stay in the country.

"That was the bank." Alex came into the room, wearing his spare uniform. He hadn't told her what had happened at the breaker's yard. He hadn't even told her about the empty office. Jack had enough on her mind. "I'm going there this afternoon," he said.

"Do you want me to come?"

"No. I'll be fine."

He came out of Liverpool Street tube station just after four-fifteen that afternoon, still wearing his school uniform: dark blue jacket, grey trousers, striped tie. He found the bank easily enough. The Royal & General occupied a tall, antique-looking building with a Union Jack fluttering from a pole about fifteen floors up. There was a brass name-plate next to the main door and a security camera swivelling slowly over the pavement.

Alex stopped in front of it. For a moment he wondered if he was making a mistake going in. If the bank had been responsible in some way for Ian Rider's death, maybe they had asked him here to arrange his own. No. The bank wouldn't kill him. He didn't even have an account there. He went in.

In an office on the seventeenth floor, the image on the security monitor flickered and changed as Street Camera #1 smoothly cut across to Reception Cameras #2 and #3 and Alex passed from the brightness outside to the cool shadows of the interior. A man sitting behind a desk reached out and pressed a button and the camera zoomed in until Alex's face filled the screen.

"So he came," the chairman of the bank muttered.

"That's the boy?" The speaker was a middle-aged woman. She had a strange, potato-shaped head and her black hair looked as if it had been cut using a pair of blunt scissors and an upturned bowl. Her eyes were almost black too. She was dressed in a severe grey suit and she was sucking a peppermint. "Are you sure about this, Alan?" she asked.

Alan Blunt nodded. "Oh yes. Quite sure. You know what to do?"

This last question was addressed to his driver,

who was standing uncomfortably, slightly hunched over. His face was a chalky white. He had been like that ever since he had tried to stop Alex in the breaker's yard. "Yes, sir," he said.

"Then do it," Blunt said. His eyes never left the screen.

In Reception, Alex had asked for John Crawley and was sitting on a leather sofa, vaguely wondering why so few people were going in or out. The reception area was wide and airy, with a brown marble floor, three elevators to one side and, above the desk, a row of clocks showing the time in every major world city. But it could have been the entrance to anywhere. A hospital. A concert hall. Even a cruise liner. The place had no identity of its own.

One of the lifts pinged open and Crawley appeared in his usual suit, but with a different tie. "I'm sorry to have kept you waiting, Alex," he said. "Have you come straight from school?"

Alex stood up but said nothing, allowing his uniform to answer the man's question.

"Let's go up to my office," Crawley said. He gestured. "We'll take the lift."

Alex didn't notice the fourth camera inside the lift, but then it was concealed on the other side of the two-way mirror that covered the back wall.

Nor did he see the thermal intensifier next to the camera. But this second machine both looked at him and through him as he stood there, turning him into a pulsating mass of different colours, none of which translated into the cold steel of a hidden gun or knife. In less than the time it took Alex to blink, the machine had passed its information down to a computer which had instantly evaluated it and then sent its own signal back to the circuits that controlled the elevator. *It's OK. He's unarmed. Continue to the fifteenth floor.*

"Here we are!" Crawley smiled and ushered Alex out into a long corridor with an uncarpeted, wooden floor and modern lighting. A series of doors was punctuated by framed paintings, brightly coloured abstracts. "My office is just along here." Crawley pointed the way.

They had passed three doors when Alex stopped. Each door had a name-plate and this one he recognized – 1504: Ian Rider. White letters on black plastic.

Crawley nodded sadly. "Yes. This was where your uncle worked. He'll be much missed."

"Can I go inside?" Alex asked.

Crawley seemed surprised. "Why do you want to do that?"

"I'd be interested to see where he worked."

"I'm sorry." Crawley sighed. "The door will have been locked and I don't have the key. Another time perhaps." He gestured again. He used his hands like a magician, as if he was about to produce a fan of cards. "I have the office next door. Just here."

They went into 1505. It was a large, square room with three windows looking out over the station. There was a flutter of red and blue outside and Alex remembered the flag he had seen. The flagpole was right next to Crawley's office. Inside there was a desk and chair, a couple of sofas, in the corner a fridge, on the wall a couple of prints. A boring executive office. Perfect for a boring executive.

"Please, Alex. Sit down," Crawley said. He went over to the fridge. "Can I get you a drink?"

"Do you have Coke?"

"Yes." Crawley opened a can and filled a glass, then handed it to Alex. "Ice?"

"No thanks." Alex took a sip. It wasn't Coke. It wasn't even Pepsi. He recognized the over-sweet, slightly cloying taste of supermarket cola and wished he'd asked for water. "So what do you want to talk to me about?"

"Your uncle's will—"

The telephone rang and with another hand-sign,

this one for "excuse me", Crawley answered it. He spoke for a few moments then hung up again. "I'm very sorry, Alex. I have to go back down to Reception. Do you mind?"

"Go ahead." Alex settled himself on the sofa.

"I'll be about five minutes." With a final nod of apology, Crawley left.

Alex waited a few seconds. Then he poured the cola into a potted plant and stood up. He went over to the door and back into the corridor. At the far end, a woman carrying a pile of papers appeared and then disappeared through a door. There was no sign of Crawley. Quickly, Alex moved back to the door of 1504 and tried the handle. But Crawley had been telling the truth. It was locked.

Alex went back into Crawley's office. He would have given anything to spend a few minutes alone in Ian Rider's office. Somebody thought the dead man's work was important enough to keep hidden from him. They had broken into his house and cleaned out everything they'd found in the office there. Perhaps the next-door room might tell him why. What exactly had Ian Rider been involved in? And was it the reason why he had been killed?

The flag fluttered again and, seeing it, Alex

went over to the window. The pole jutted out of the building exactly halfway between rooms 1504 and 1505. If he could somehow reach it, he should be able to jump on to the ledge that ran along the side of the building outside room 1504. Of course, he was fifteen floors up. If he jumped and missed there would be about seventy metres to fall. It was a stupid idea. It wasn't even worth thinking about.

Alex opened the window and climbed out. It was better not to think about it at all. He would just do it. After all, if this had been the ground floor, or a climbing-frame in the school yard, it would have been child's play. It was only the sheer brick wall stretching down to the pavement, the cars and buses moving like toys so far below and the blast of the wind against his face that made it terrifying. Don't think about it. Do it.

Alex lowered himself on to the ledge outside Crawley's office. His hands were behind him, clutching on to the window-sill. He took a deep breath. And jumped.

A camera located in an office across the road caught Alex as he launched himself into space. Two floors above, Alan Blunt was still sitting in front of the screen. He chuckled. It was a humourless sound. "I told you," he said. "The boy's extraordinary."

"The boy's quite mad," the woman retorted.

"Well, maybe that's what we need."

"You're just going to sit here and watch him kill himself?"

"I'm going to sit here and hope he survives."

Alex had miscalculated the jump. He had missed the flagpole by a centimetre and would have plunged down to the pavement if his hands hadn't caught hold of the Union Jack itself. He was hanging now with his feet in mid-air. Slowly, with huge effort, he pulled himself up, his fingers hooking into the material. Somehow he managed to climb back up on to the pole. He still didn't look down. He just hoped that no passer-by would look up.

It was easier after that. He squatted on the pole, then threw himself across to the ledge outside Ian Rider's office. He had to be careful. Too far to the left and he would crash into the side of the building, but too far the other way and he would fall. In fact he landed perfectly, grabbing hold of the ledge with both hands and then pulling himself up until he was level with the window. It was only then that he wondered if the window would be locked. If so, he'd just have to go back.

It wasn't. Alex slid the window open and hoisted himself into the second office, which was in many ways a carbon copy of the first. It had the same furniture, the same carpet, even a similar print on the wall. He went over to the desk and sat down. The first thing he saw was a photograph of himself, taken the summer before on the Caribbean island of Guadeloupe, where he had gone diving. There was a second picture tucked into the corner of the frame. Alex aged five or six. He was surprised by the photographs. He had never thought of Ian Rider as a sentimental man.

Alex glanced at his watch. About three minutes had passed since Crawley had left the office, and he had said he would be back in five. If he was going to find anything here, he had to find it quickly. He pulled open a drawer of the desk. It contained five or six thick files. Alex took them and opened them. He saw at once that they had nothing to do with banking.

The first was marked: NERVE POISONS – NEW METHODS OF CONCEALMENT AND DISSEMINA- TION. Alex put it aside and looked at the second. ASSASSINATIONS – FOUR CASE STUDIES. Growing ever more puzzled, he quickly flicked through the rest of the files, which covered counter-terrorism, the movement of uranium across Europe and interrogation techniques. The last file was simply labelled: STORMBREAKER.

Alex was about to read it when the door suddenly opened and two men walked in. One of them was Crawley. The other was the driver from the breaker's yard. Alex knew there was no point trying to explain what he was doing. He was sitting behind the desk with the Stormbreaker file open in his hands. But at the same time he realized that the two men weren't surprised to see him there. From the way they had come into the room, they had expected to find him.

"This isn't a bank," Alex said. "Who are you? Was my uncle working for you? Did you kill him?"

"So many questions," Crawley muttered. "But I'm afraid we're not authorized to give you the answers."

The other man lifted his hand and Alex saw that he was holding a gun. He stood up behind the desk, holding the file as if to protect himself. "No—" he began.

The man fired. There was no explosion. The gun spat at Alex and he felt something slam into his heart. His hand opened and the file tumbled to the ground. Then his legs buckled, the room twisted and he fell back into nothing.

"SO WHAT DO YOU SAY?"

Alex opened his eyes. So he was still alive! That was a nice surprise.

He was lying on a bed in a large, comfortable room. The bed was modern but the room was old, with beams running across the ceiling, a stone fireplace and narrow windows in ornate wooden frames. He had seen rooms like this in books when he was studying Shakespeare. He would have said the building was Elizabethan. It had to be somewhere in the country. There was no sound of traffic. Outside he could see trees.

Someone had undressed him. His school uniform was gone. Instead he was wearing loose pyjamas, silk from the feel of them. From the light outside he would have guessed it was early evening. He found his watch lying on the table beside the bed and he reached out for it. The time was twelve o'clock. It had been half-past four when he was shot with what must have been a drugged dart. He had lost a whole night and half a day.

There was a bathroom leading off the bedroom; bright white tiles and a huge shower behind a cylinder of glass and chrome. Alex stripped off the pyjamas and stood for five minutes under a jet of steaming water. He felt better after that.

He went back into the bedroom and opened the cupboard. Someone had been to his house in Chelsea. All his clothes were here, neatly hung up. He wondered what Crawley had told Jack. Presumably he would have made up some story to explain his sudden disappearance. He took out a pair of Gap combat trousers, a Nike sweatshirt and trainers, got dressed, then sat on the bed and waited.

About fifteen minutes later there was a knock and the door opened. A young Asian woman in a nurse's uniform came in, beaming.

"Oh, you're awake. And dressed. How are you feeling? Not too groggy, I hope. Please come this way. Mr Blunt is expecting you for lunch."

Alex hadn't spoken a word to her. He followed her out of the room, along a corridor and down a flight of stairs. The house was indeed Elizabethan, with wooden panels along the corridors, ornate chandeliers and oil paintings of old, bearded men in tunics and ruffs. The stairs led down into a tall, galleried room with a rug spread out over flagstones and a fireplace big enough to park a car in. A long, polished wooden table had been laid for three. Alan Blunt and a dark, rather masculine woman unwrapping a sweet were already sitting down. Mrs Blunt?

"Alex." Blunt smiled briefly, as if it was something he didn't enjoy doing. "It's good of you to join us."

Alex sat down. "You didn't give me a lot of choice."

"Yes. I don't quite know what Crawley was thinking of, shooting you like that, but I suppose it was the easiest way. May I introduce my colleague, Mrs Jones."

The woman nodded at Alex. Her eyes seemed to examine him minutely, but she said nothing.

"Who are you?" Alex asked. "What do you want with me?"

"I'm sure you have a great many questions. But first, let's eat." Blunt must have pressed a hidden button, or else he was being overheard, for at that precise moment a door opened and a waiter

– in white jacket and black trousers – appeared carrying three plates. "I hope you eat meat," Blunt continued. "Today it's *carré d'agneau*."

"You mean, roast lamb."

"The chef is French."

Alex waited until the food had been served. Blunt and Mrs Jones drank red wine. He stuck to water. Finally, Blunt began.

"As I'm sure you've gathered," he said, "the Royal & General is not a bank. In fact it doesn't exist ... it's nothing more than a cover. And it follows, of course, that your uncle had nothing to do with banking. He worked for me. My name, as I told you at the funeral, is Blunt. I am Chief Executive of the Special Operations Division of MI6. And your uncle was, for want of a better word, a spy."

Alex couldn't help smiling. "You mean ... like James Bond?"

"Similar, although we don't go in for numbers. Double O and all the rest of it. He was a field agent, highly trained and very courageous. He successfully completed assignments in Iran, Washington, Hong Kong and Cairo – to name but a few. I imagine this must come as a bit of a shock to you."

Alex thought about the dead man, what he had

known of him. His privacy. His long absences abroad. And the times he had come home injured. A bandaged arm one time. A bruised face another. Little accidents, Alex had been told. But now it all made sense. "I'm not shocked," he said.

Blunt cut a neat slice of meat. "Ian Rider's luck ran out on his last mission," he went on. "He had been working undercover here in England, in Cornwall, and was driving back to London to make a report when he was killed. You saw his car at the yard."

"Stryker & Son," Alex muttered. "Who are they?"

"Just people we use. We have budget restraints. We have to contract some of our work out. Mrs Jones here is our Head of Special Operations. She gave your uncle his last assignment."

"We're very sorry to have lost him, Alex." The woman spoke for the first time. She didn't sound very sorry at all.

"Do you know who killed him?"

"Yes."

"Are you going to tell me?"

"No. Not now."

"Why not?"

"Because you don't need to know. Not at this stage."

"All right." Alex put down his knife and fork. He hadn't actually eaten anything. "My uncle was a spy. Thanks to you he's dead. I found out too much, so you knocked me out and brought me here. Where am I, by the way?"

"This is one of our training centres," Mrs Jones said.

"You've brought me here because you don't want me to tell anyone what I know. Is that what this is all about? Because if it is, I'll sign the Official Secrets Act or whatever it is you want me to do, but then I'd like to go home. This is all crazy anyway. And I've had enough. I'm out of here."

Blunt coughed quietly. "It's not quite as easy as that," he said.

"Why not?"

"It's certainly true that you did draw attention to yourself both at the breaker's yard and then at our offices on Liverpool Street. And it's also true that what you know and what I'm about to tell you must go no further. But the fact of the matter is, Alex, we need your help."

"My help?"

"Yes." He paused. "Have you heard of a man called Herod Sayle?"

Alex thought for a moment. "I've seen his name in the newspapers. He's something to do with computers. And he owns racehorses. Doesn't he come from somewhere in Egypt?"

"No. From the Lebanon." Blunt took a sip of wine. "Let me tell you his story, Alex. I'm sure you'll find it of interest...

"Herod Sayle was born in complete poverty in the back streets of Beirut. His father was a failed hairdresser. His mother took in washing. He had nine brothers and four sisters, all living together in three small rooms along with the family goat. Young Herod never went to school and he should have ended up unemployed, unable to read or write, like the rest of his family.

"But when he was seven, something occurred that changed his life. He was walking down Olive Street, in the middle of Beirut, when he happened to see an upright piano fall out of a fourteenth-storey window. Apparently it was being moved and it somehow overturned. Anyway, there were a couple of American tourists walking along the pavement below and they would both have been crushed – no doubt about it – except that at the last minute Herod threw himself at them and pushed them out of the way. The piano missed them by a millimetre.

"Of course, they were enormously grateful to the young waif, and it now turned out that they were very rich. They made enquiries about him and discovered how poor he was ... the very clothes he was wearing had been passed down by all nine of his brothers. And so, out of gratitude, they more or less adopted him. Flew him out of Beirut and put him into a school over here, where he made astonishing progress. He got nine O-levels and – here's an amazing coincidence – at the age of fifteen he actually found himself sitting next to a boy who would grow up to become Prime Minister of Great Britain. Our present Prime Minister, in fact. The two of them were at school together.

"I'll move quickly forward. After school, Sayle went to Cambridge, where he got a first in Economics. He then set out on a career that went from success to success. His own radio station, record label, computer software ... and, yes, he even found time to buy a string of racehorses, although for some reason they always seem to come last. But what drew him to our attention was his most recent invention. A quite revolutionary computer which he calls the Stormbreaker."

Stormbreaker. Alex remembered the file he had

found in Ian Rider's office. Things were beginning to come together.

"The Stormbreaker is being manufactured by Sayle Enterprises," Mrs Jones said. "There's been a lot of talk about the design. It has a black keyboard and black casing—"

"With a lightning bolt going down the side," Alex said. He had seen a picture of it online.

"It doesn't only look different," Blunt cut in. "It's based on a completely new technology. It uses something called the round processor. I don't suppose that will mean anything to you."

"It's an integrated circuit on a sphere of silicon about one millimetre in diameter," Alex said. "It's ninety per cent cheaper to produce than an ordinary chip because the whole thing is sealed in, so you don't need clean rooms for production."

"Oh. Yes..." Blunt coughed. "Well, the point is, later today, Sayle Enterprises are going to make a quite remarkable announcement. They are planning to give away tens of thousands of these computers. In fact, it is their intention to ensure that every secondary school in Britain gets its own Stormbreaker. It's an unparalleled act of generosity, Sayle's way of thanking the country that gave him a home."

"So the man's a hero."

"So it would seem. He wrote to Downing Street a few months ago:

"My Dear Prime Minister

You may remember me from our school-days together. For almost forty years I have lived in England and I wish to make a gesture, something that will never be forgotten, to express my true feelings towards your country.

"The letter went on to describe the gift and was signed *Yours humbly,* by the man himself. Of course, the whole Government was cock-a-hoop.

"The computers are being assembled at the Sayle plant down in Port Tallon, Cornwall. They'll be shipped across the country at the end of this month and on April 1st there's to be a special ceremony at the Science Museum in London. The Prime Minister is going to press the button that will bring all the computers on-line ... the whole lot of them. And – this is top secret by the way – Mr Sayle is to be rewarded with British citizenship, which is apparently something he has always wanted."

"Well, I'm very happy for him," Alex said. "But you still haven't told me what this has got to do with me."

Blunt glanced at Mrs Jones, who had finished

her meal while he was talking. She unwrapped another peppermint and took over.

"For some time now, our department – Special Operations – has been concerned about Mr Sayle. The fact of the matter is, we've been wondering if he isn't too good to be true. I won't go into all the details, Alex, but we've been looking at his business dealings ... he has contacts in China and the former Soviet Union; countries that have never been our friends. The Government may think he's a saint, but there's a ruthless side to him too. And the security arrangements down at Port Tallon worry us. He's more or less got his own private army. He's acting as if he's got something to hide."

"Not that anyone will listen," Blunt muttered.

"Exactly. The Government's too keen to get their hands on these computers to listen to us. That was why we decided to send our own man down to the plant. Supposedly to check on security. But in fact his job was to keep an eye on Herod Sayle."

"You're talking about my uncle," Alex said. Ian Rider had told him that he was going to an insurance convention. Another lie in a life that had been nothing but lies.

"Yes. He was there for three weeks and,

like us, he didn't exactly take to Mr Sayle. In his first reports, he described him as short-tempered and unpleasant. But at the same time, he had to admit that everything seemed to be fine. Production was on schedule. The Stormbreakers were coming off the line. And everyone seemed to be happy.

"But then we got a message. Rider couldn't say very much because it was an open line, but he told us that something had happened. He said he'd discovered something. That the Stormbreakers mustn't leave the plant and that he was coming up to London at once. He left Port Tallon at four o'clock. He never even got to the motorway. He was ambushed in a quiet country lane. The local police found the car. We arranged for it to be brought up here."

Alex sat in silence. He could imagine it. A twisting lane with the trees just in blossom. The silver BMW gleaming as it raced past. And, round a corner, a second car waiting... "Why are you telling me all this?" he asked.

"It proves what we were saying," Blunt replied. "We have our doubts about Sayle, so we send a man down. Our best man. He finds out something and he ends up dead. Maybe Rider discovered the truth —"

"But I don't understand!" Alex interrupted. "Sayle is giving away the computers. He's not making any money out of them. In return he's getting British citizenship. Fine! What's he got to hide?"

"We don't know," Blunt said. "We just don't know. But we want to find out. And soon. Before these computers leave the plant."

"They're being shipped out on 31st March," Mrs Jones added. "Only about two weeks from now." She glanced at Blunt. He nodded. "That's why it's essential for us to send someone else to Port Tallon. Someone to continue where your uncle left off."

Alex smiled queasily. "I hope you're not looking at me."

"We can't just send in another agent," Mrs Jones said. "The enemy has shown his hand. He's killed Rider. He'll be expecting a replacement. Somehow we have to trick him."

"We have to send in someone who won't be noticed," Blunt continued. "Someone who can look around and report back without being seen themselves. We were considering sending down a woman. She might be able to slip in as a secretary or receptionist. But then I had a better idea.

"A few months ago, one of these computer

magazines ran a competition. *Be the first boy or girl to use the Stormbreaker. Travel to Port Tallon and meet Herod Sayle himself.* That was the first prize – and it was won by some young chap who's apparently a bit of a whizz-kid when it comes to computers. Name of Felix Lester. Fourteen years old. The same age as you. He looks a bit like you too. He's expected down at Port Tallon less than two weeks from now."

"Wait a minute—"

"You've already shown yourself to be extraordinarily brave and resourceful," Blunt said. "First of all at the breaker's yard ... that was a karate kick, wasn't it? How long have you been learning karate?" Alex didn't answer, so he went on. "And then there was that little test we arranged for you at the bank. Any boy who would climb out of a fifteenth-floor window just to satisfy his own curiosity has to be rather special, and it seems to me that you are very special indeed."

"What we're suggesting is that you come and work for us," Mrs Jones said. "We have enough time to give you some basic training – not that you'll need it, probably – and we can equip you with a few items that may help you with what we have in mind. Then we'll arrange for you to take the place of this other boy. You'll go to Sayle

Enterprises on 29th March. That's when this Lester boy is expected. You'll stay there until 1st April, which is the day of the ceremony. The timing couldn't be better. You'll be able to meet Herod Sayle, keep an eye on him and tell us what you think. Perhaps you'll also find out what it was that your uncle discovered and why he had to die. You shouldn't be in any danger. After all, who would suspect a fourteen-year-old boy of being a spy?"

"All we're asking you to do is report back to us," Blunt said. "That's all we want. Two weeks of your time. A chance to make sure these computers are everything they're cracked up to be. A chance to serve your country."

Blunt had finished his dinner. His plate was completely clean, as if there had never been any food on it at all. He put down his knife and fork, laying them precisely side by side. "All right, Alex," he said. "So what do you say?"

There was a long pause.

Blunt was watching him with polite interest. Mrs Jones was unwrapping yet another peppermint, her black eyes seemingly fixed on the twist of paper in her hands.

"No," Alex said.

"I'm sorry?"

"It's a dumb idea. I don't want to be a spy. I want to be a footballer. Anyway, I have a life of my own." He found it difficult to choose the right words. The whole thing was so preposterous he almost wanted to laugh. "Why don't you ask this Felix Lester to snoop around for you?"

"We don't believe he'd be as resourceful as you," Blunt said.

"He's probably better at computer games." Alex shook his head. "I'm sorry. I'm just not interested. I don't want to get involved."

"That's a pity," Blunt said. His tone of voice hadn't changed but there was a heavy, dead quality to the words. And there was something different, too, about him. Throughout the meal he had been polite; not friendly, but at least human. In an instant, that had disappeared. Alex thought of a toilet chain being pulled. The human part of him had just been flushed away.

"Then we'd better move on to discuss your future," he continued. "Like it or not, Alex, the Royal & General is now your legal guardian."

"I thought you said the Royal & General didn't exist."

Blunt ignored him. "Ian Rider has of course left the house and all his money to you. However, he left it in trust until you are twenty-one. And we control that trust. So there will, I'm afraid, have to be some changes. The American girl who lives with you."

"Jack?"

"Miss Starbright. Her visa has expired. She'll be returned to America. We propose to put the house on the market. Unfortunately, you have no relatives to look after you, so I'm afraid that also means you'll have to leave Brookland. You'll be sent to an institution. There's one I know just outside Birmingham. The Saint Elizabeth in Sourbridge. Not a very pleasant place, but I'm afraid there's no alternative."

"You're blackmailing me!" Alex exclaimed.

"Not at all."

"But if I agree to do what you ask...?"

Blunt glanced at Mrs Jones. "Help us and we'll help you," she said.

Alex considered, but not for very long. He had no choice and he knew it. Not when these people controlled his money, his present life, his entire future. "You talked about training," he said.

Mrs Jones nodded. "That's why we brought you here, Alex. This is a training centre. If you agree to what we want, we can start at once."

"Start at once." Alex spoke the three words without liking the sound of them. Blunt and Mrs

Jones were waiting for his answer. He sighed. "Yeah. All right. It doesn't look like I've got very much choice."

He glanced at the slices of cold lamb on his plate. Dead meat. Suddenly he knew how it felt.

DOUBLE O NOTHING

For the hundredth time, Alex cursed Alan Blunt using language he hadn't even realized he knew. It was almost five o'clock in the evening, although it could have been five o'clock in the morning: the sky had barely changed at all throughout the day. It was grey, cold, unforgiving. The rain was still falling, a thin drizzle that travelled horizontally in the wind, soaking through his supposedly waterproof clothing, mixing with his sweat and his dirt, chilling him to the bone.

He unfolded his map and checked his position once again. He had to be close to the last RV of the day – the last rendezvous point – but he could see nothing. He was standing on a narrow track made up of loose grey shingle that crunched under his combat boots when he walked. The track snaked round the side of a mountain with a sheer drop to the right. He was somewhere in the Brecon Beacons and there should have been a view, but it had been wiped out by the rain and the fading light. A few trees twisted out of the side of the hill, with leaves as hard as thorns. Behind him, below him, ahead of him, it was all the same. Nowhere Land.

Alex hurt. The 10-kilogram Bergen rucksack he had been forced to wear cut into his shoulders and had rubbed blisters on his back. His right knee, where he had fallen earlier in the day, was no longer bleeding but still stung. His shoulder was bruised and there was a gash along the side of his neck. His camouflage outfit – he had swapped his Gap combat trousers for the real thing – fitted him badly, cutting his legs and under his arms but hanging loose everywhere else. He was close to exhaustion, he knew, almost too tired to feel how much pain he was in. But for the glucose and caffeine tablets in his survival pack, he would have ground to a halt hours ago. He knew that if he didn't find the RV soon, he would be physically unable to continue. Then he would be thrown off the course. "Binned" as they called it. They would like that. Swallowing down the taste of defeat, Alex folded the map and forced himself on.

It was his ninth – or maybe his tenth – day of training. Time had begun to dissolve into itself, as shapeless as the rain. After his lunch with Alan Blunt and Mrs Jones, he had been moved out of the manor house and into a crude wooden hut in the training camp a few miles away. There were nine huts in total, each equipped with four metal beds and four metal lockers. A fifth had been squeezed into one of them to accommodate Alex. Two more huts, painted a different colour, stood side by side. One of these was a kitchen and mess hall. The other contained toilets, sinks and showers – with not a single hot tap in sight.

On his first day there, Alex had been introduced to his training officer, an incredibly fit black sergeant. He was the sort of man who thought he'd seen everything. Until he saw Alex. And he had examined the new arrival for a long minute before he had spoken.

"It's not my job to ask questions," he had said. "But if it was, I'd want to know what they're thinking of, sending me children. Do you have any idea where you are, boy? This isn't Center Parcs. This isn't the Club Méditerranée." He cut the word into its five syllables and spat them out. "I have you for eleven days and they expect me to give you the sort of training that should take fourteen weeks. That's not just mad. That's suicidal."

"I didn't ask to be here," Alex had said.

Suddenly the sergeant was furious. "You don't speak to me unless I give you permission," he shouted. "And when you speak to me, you address me as 'sir'. Do you understand?"

"Yes, sir." Alex had already decided that the man was even worse than his geography teacher.

"There are five units operational here at the moment," the officer went on. "You'll join K Unit. We don't use names. I have no name. You have no name. If anyone asks you what you're doing, you tell them nothing. Some of the men may be hard on you. Some of them may resent you being here. That's too bad. You'll just have to live with it. And there's something else you need to know. I can make allowances for you. You're a boy, not a man. But if you complain, you'll be binned. If you cry, you'll be binned. If you can't keep up, you'll be binned. Between you and me, boy, this is a mistake and I want to bin you."

After that, Alex joined K Unit. As the sergeant had predicted, they weren't exactly overjoyed to see him.

There were four of them. As Alex was soon to

discover, the Special Operations Division of MI6 sent its agents to the same training centre used by the Special Air Service – the SAS. Much of the training was based on SAS methods and this included the numbers and make-up of each team. So there were four men, each with their own special skills. And one boy, seemingly with none.

They were all in their mid-twenties, spread out over the bunks in companionable silence. Two of them smoking. One dismantling and reassembling his gun – a 9mm Browning High Power pistol. Each of them had been given a codename: Wolf, Fox, Eagle and Snake. From now on, Alex would be known as Cub. The leader, Wolf, was the one with the gun. He was short and muscular with square shoulders and black, close-cropped hair. He had a handsome face, made slightly uneven by his nose, which had been broken at some time in the past.

He was the first to speak. Putting the gun down, he examined Alex with cold, dark-grey eyes. "So who the hell do you think you are?" he demanded.

"Cub," Alex replied.

"A bloody schoolboy!" Wolf spoke with a strange, slightly foreign accent. "I don't believe it. Are you with Special Operations?"

"I'm not allowed to tell you that." Alex went over to his bunk and sat down. The mattress felt as solid as the frame. Despite the cold, there was only one blanket.

Wolf shook his head and smiled humourlessly. "Look what they've sent us," he muttered. "Double O Seven? Double O Nothing more like."

After that, the name stuck. Double O Nothing was what they called him.

In the days that followed, Alex shadowed the group, not quite part of it but never far away. Almost everything they did, he did. He learned map-reading, radio communication and first aid. He took part in an unarmed combat class and was knocked to the ground so often that it took all his nerve to persuade himself to get up again.

And then there was the assault course. Five times he was shouted and bullied across the nightmare of nets and ladders, tunnels and ditches, swinging tightropes and towering walls, that stretched for almost half a kilometre through, and over, the woodland beside the huts. Alex thought of it as the adventure play-ground from hell. The first time he tried it, he fell off a rope and into a pit that seemed to have been filled on purpose with freezing slime. Half-drowned and filthy, he had been sent back to the start by the sergeant. Alex thought he would never get to the end, but the second time he finished it in twenty-five minutes – which he cut to seventeen minutes by the end of the week. Bruised and exhausted though he was, he was quietly pleased with himself. Even Wolf only managed it in twelve.

Wolf remained actively hostile towards Alex. The other three men simply ignored him, but Wolf did everything he could to taunt or humiliate him. It was as if Alex had somehow insulted him by being placed in the group. Once, crawling under the nets, Wolf lashed out with his foot, missing Alex's face by a centimetre. Of course he would have said it was an accident if the boot had connected. Another time he was more successful, tripping Alex up in the mess hall and sending him flying, along with his tray, cutlery and steaming plate of stew. And every time he spoke to Alex, he used the same sneering tone of voice.

"Goodnight, Double O Nothing. Don't wet the bed."

Alex bit his lip and said nothing. But he was glad when the four men were sent off for a day's jungle survival course – this wasn't part of his own training – even though the sergeant worked him twice as hard once they were gone. He preferred to be on his own.

But on the eighth day, Wolf did come close to finishing him altogether. It happened in the Killing House.

The Killing House was a fake; a mock-up of an embassy used to train the SAS in the art of hostage release. Alex had twice watched K Unit go into the house, the first time swinging down from the roof, and had followed their progress on CCTV. All four men were armed. Alex himself didn't take part because someone somewhere had decided he shouldn't carry a gun. Inside the Killing House, mannequins had been arranged as terrorists and hostages. Smashing down the doors and using stun grenades to clear the rooms with deafening, multiple blasts, Wolf, Fox, Eagle and Snake had successfully completed their mission both times.

This time Alex had joined them. The Killing House had been booby-trapped. They weren't told how. All five of them were unarmed. Their job was simply to get from one end of the house to the other without being "killed".

They almost made it. In the first room, made up to look like a huge dining-room, they found the pressure pads under the carpet and the infrared beams across the doors. For Alex it was an eerie experience, tiptoeing behind the other four men, watching as they dismantled the two devices, using cigarette smoke to expose the otherwise invisible beams. It was strange to be afraid of everything and yet see nothing. In the hallway there was a motion detector which would have activated a machine-gun (Alex assumed it was loaded with blanks) behind a Japanese screen. The third room was empty. The fourth was a living-room with the exit – a set of french windows – on the other side. There was a trip-wire, barely thicker than a human hair, running the entire width of the room, and the french windows were alarmed. While Snake dealt with the alarm, Fox and Eagle prepared to neutralize the trip-wire, unclipping an electronic circuit board and a variety of tools from their belts.

Wolf stopped them. "Leave it. We're out of here." At the same moment, Snake signalled. He had deactivated the alarm. The french windows were open.

Snake was the first out. Then Fox and Eagle. Alex would have been the last to leave the room, but just as he reached the exit he found Wolf blocking his way.

"Tough luck, Double O Nothing," Wolf said. His voice was soft, almost kind.

The next thing Alex knew, the heel of Wolf's

palm had rammed into his chest, pushing him back with astonishing force. Taken by surprise, he lost his balance and fell, remembered the trip-wire and tried to twist his body to avoid it. But it was hopeless. His flailing left hand caught the wire. He actually felt it against his wrist. He hit the floor, pulling the wire with him. And then...

The HRT stun grenade has been used frequently by the SAS. It's a small device filled with a mixture of magnesium powder and mercury fulminate. When the trip-wire activated the grenade, the mercury exploded at once, not just deafening Alex but shuddering through him as if it could rip out his heart. At the same time, the magnesium ignited and burned for a full ten seconds. The light was so blinding that even closing his eyes made no difference. Alex lay there with his face against the hard wooden floor, his hands scrabbling against his head, unable to move, waiting for it to end.

But even then it wasn't over. When the magnesium finally burned out, it was as if all the light had burned out with it. Alex stumbled to his feet, unable to see or hear, not even sure any more where he was. He felt sick to his stomach. The room swayed around him. The heavy smell of chemicals hung in the air.

Ten minutes later he staggered out into the open. Wolf was waiting for him with the others, his face blank, and Alex realized he must have slipped out before he'd hit the ground. An angry sergeant walked over to him. Alex hadn't expected to see a shred of concern in the man's face and he wasn't disappointed.

"Do you want to tell me what happened in there, Cub?" he demanded. When Alex didn't answer, he went on. "You ruined the exercise. You fouled up. You could get the whole unit binned. So you'd better start telling me what went wrong."

Alex glanced at Wolf. Wolf looked the other way. What should he say? Should he even try to tell the truth?

"Well?" The sergeant was waiting.

"Nothing happened, sir," Alex said. "I just wasn't looking where I was going. I stepped on something and there was an explosion."

"If that was real life, you'd be dead," the sergeant said. "What did I tell you? Sending me a child was a mistake. And a stupid, clumsy child who doesn't look where he's going ... that's even worse!"

Alex stood where he was, just taking it. Out of the corner of his eye, he could see Wolf half-smiling.

The sergeant had seen it too. "You think it's so funny, Wolf? You can go clean up in there. And tonight you'd better get some rest. All of you. Because tomorrow you've got a forty kilometre hike. Survival rations. No fire. This is a survival course. And if you do survive, then maybe you'll have a reason to smile."

Alex remembered the words now, exactly twenty-four hours later. He had spent the last eleven of them on his feet, following the trail the sergeant had set out for him on the map. The exercise had begun at six o'clock in the morning after a grey-lit breakfast of sausages and beans. Wolf and the others had disappeared into the distance ahead of him a long time ago, even though they had been given 25-kilogram rucksacks to carry. They had also been given only eight hours to complete the course. Allowing for his age, Alex had been given twelve.

He rounded a corner, his feet scrunching on the gravel. There was someone standing ahead of him. It was the sergeant. He had just lit a cigarette and Alex watched him slide the matches back into his pocket. Seeing him there brought back the shame and the anger of the day before and at the same time sapped the last of his strength. Suddenly Alex had had enough of Blunt, Mrs Jones, Wolf ... the whole stupid thing. With a final effort he stumbled the last hundred metres and came to a halt. Rain and sweat trickled down the side of his face. His hair, now dark with grime, was glued across his forehead.

The sergeant looked at his watch. "Eleven hours, five minutes. That's not bad, Cub. But the others were here three hours ago."

Bully for them, Alex thought. He didn't say anything.

"Anyway, you should just make it to the last RV," the sergeant went on. "It's up there."

He pointed to a wall. Not a sloping wall. A sheer one. Solid rock rising fifty metres up without a handhold or a foothold in sight. Even looking at it, Alex felt his stomach shrink. Ian Rider had taken him climbing – in Scotland, in France, all over Europe. But he had never attempted anything as difficult as this. Not on his own. Not when he was so tired.

"I can't," he said. In the end the two words came out easily.

"I didn't hear that," the sergeant said.

"I said, I can't do it, sir."

"Can't isn't a word we use around here."

"I don't care. I've had enough. I've just had..."

Alex's voice cracked. He didn't trust himself to go on. He stood there, cold and empty, waiting for the axe to fall.

But it didn't. The sergeant gazed at him for a long minute. He nodded his head slowly. "Listen to me, Cub," he said. "I know what happened in the Killing House."

Alex glanced up.

"Wolf forgot about the CCTV. We've got it all on film."

"Then why—?" Alex began.

"Did you make a complaint against him, Cub?"

"No, sir."

"Do you want to make a complaint against him, Cub?"

A pause. Then, "No, sir."

"Good." The sergeant pointed at the rock face, suggesting a path up with his finger. "It's not as difficult as it looks," he said. "And they're waiting for you just over the top. You've got a nice cold dinner. Survival rations. You don't want to miss that."

Alex drew a deep breath and started forward. As he passed the sergeant, he stumbled and put out a hand to steady himself, brushing against him. "Sorry, sir," he said.

It took him twenty minutes to reach the top

and, sure enough, K Unit was already there, crouching around three small tents that they must have pitched earlier in the afternoon. Two for two men sharing. One, the smallest, for Alex.

Snake, a thin, fair-haired man who spoke with a Scottish accent, looked up at Alex. He had a tin of cold stew in one hand, a teaspoon in the other.

"I didn't think you'd make it," he said. Alex couldn't help but notice a certain warmth in the man's voice. And for the first time he hadn't called him Double O Nothing.

"Nor did I," Alex said.

Wolf was squatting over what he hoped would become a camp-fire, trying to get it started with two flints while Fox and Eagle watched. He was getting nowhere. The stones only produced the smallest of sparks, and the scraps of newspaper and leaves that he had collected were already far too wet. Wolf struck at the stones again and again. The others watched, their faces glum.

Alex held out the box of matches that he had pick-pocketed from the sergeant when he had pretended to stumble at the foot of the rock face.

"These might help," he said.

He threw the matches down, then went into his tent.

TOYS AREN'T US

In the London office, Mrs Jones sat waiting while Alan Blunt read the report. The sun was shining. A pigeon was strutting back and forth along the ledge outside as if keeping guard.

"He's doing very well," Blunt said at last. "Remarkably well, in fact." He turned a page. "I see he missed target practice."

"Were you planning to give him a gun?" Mrs Jones asked.

"No. I don't think that would be a good idea."

"Then why does he need target practice?"

Blunt raised an eyebrow. "We can't give a teenager a gun," he said. "On the other hand, I don't think we can send him to Port Tallon empty-handed. You'd better have a word with Smithers."

"I already have. He's working on it now."

Mrs Jones stood up as if to leave. But at the door she hesitated. "I wonder if it's occurred to you that Rider may have been preparing him for this all along," she said.

"What do you mean?"

"Preparing Alex to replace him. Ever since the boy was old enough to walk, he's been in training for intelligence work ... but without knowing it. I mean, he's lived abroad, so he now speaks French, German and Spanish. He's been mountain-climbing, diving and skiing. He's learned karate. Physically he's in perfect shape." She shrugged. "I think Rider wanted Alex to become a spy."

"But not so soon," Blunt said.

"I agree. You know as well as I do, Alan – he's not ready yet. If we send him into Sayle Enterprises, he's going to get himself killed."

"Perhaps." The single word was cold, matter-of-fact.

"He's fourteen years old! We can't do it."

"We have to." Blunt stood up and opened the window, letting in the air and the sound of the traffic. The pigeon hurled itself off the ledge, afraid of him. "This whole business worries me," he said. "The Prime Minister sees the Storm-breakers as a major coup, for himself and for his

Government. But there's still something about Herod Sayle that I don't like. Did you tell the boy about Yassen Gregorovich?"

"No." Mrs Jones shook her head.

"Then it's time you did. It was Yassen who killed his uncle. I'm sure of it. And if Yassen was working for Sayle—"

"What will you do if Yassen kills Alex Rider?"

"That's not our problem, Mrs Jones. If the boy gets himself killed, it will be the final proof that there is something wrong. At the very least it'll allow me to postpone the Stormbreaker project and take a good, hard look at what's going on at Port Tallon. In a way, it would almost help us if he *was* killed."

"The boy's not ready yet. He'll make mistakes. It won't take them long to find out who he is." Mrs Jones sighed. "I don't think Alex has got much chance at all."

"I agree." Blunt turned back from the window. The sun slanted over his shoulder. A single shadow fell across his face. "But it's too late to worry about that now," he said. "We have no more time. Stop the training. Send him in."

Alex sat hunched up in the back of the low-flying C-130 military aircraft, his stomach churning behind his knees. There were twelve men sitting in two lines around him – his own unit and two others. For an hour now, the plane had been flying at just one hundred metres, following the Welsh valleys, dipping and swerving to avoid the mountain peaks. A single bulb glowed red behind a wire mesh, adding to the heat in the cramped cabin. Alex could feel the engines vibrating through him. It was like travelling in a tumble-drier and microwave oven combined.

The thought of jumping out of a plane with an oversized silk umbrella would have made Alex sick with fear – but only that morning he'd been told that he wouldn't in fact be jumping himself. A signal from London. They couldn't risk him breaking a leg, it said, and Alex guessed that the end of his training was near. Even so, he'd been taught how to pack a parachute, how to control it, how to exit a plane and how to land, and at the end of the day the sergeant had instructed him to join the flight – just for the experience. Now, close to the drop zone, Alex felt almost disappointed. He'd watch everyone else jump and then he'd be left alone.

"P minus five..."

The voice of the pilot came over the speaker system, distant and metallic. Alex gritted his teeth. Five minutes until the jump. He looked at the other men, shuffling into position, checking the cords that connected them to the static line. He was sitting next to Wolf. To his surprise, the man was completely quiet, unmoving. It was hard to tell in the half-darkness, but the look on his face could almost have been fear.

There was a loud buzz and the red light turned green. The assistant pilot had climbed through from the cockpit. He reached for a handle and pulled open a door set in the back of the aircraft, allowing the cold air to rush in. Alex could see a single square of night. It was raining. The rain howled past.

The green light began to flash. The assistant pilot tapped the first pair on their shoulders and Alex watched them shuffle over to the side and then throw themselves out. For a moment they were there, frozen in the doorway. Then they were gone, like a photograph crumpled and spun away by the wind. Two more men followed. Then another two, until only the final pair had still to jump.

Alex glanced at Wolf, who seemed to be struggling with a piece of equipment. His partner was moving to the door without him, but still Wolf didn't look up.

The other man jumped. Suddenly Alex was aware that only he and Wolf were left.

"Move it!" the assistant pilot shouted above the roar of the engines.

Wolf picked himself up. His eyes briefly met Alex's and in that moment Alex knew. Wolf was a popular leader. He was tough and he was fast, completing a forty-kilometre hike as if it was just a stroll in the park. But he had a weak spot. Somehow he'd allowed this parachute jump to get to him and he was too scared to move. It was hard to believe, but there he was, frozen in the doorway, his arms rigid, staring out. Alex glanced back. The assistant pilot was looking the other way. He hadn't seen what was happening. And when he did? If Wolf failed to make the jump, it would be the end of his training and maybe even the end of his career. Even hesitating would be bad enough. He'd be binned.

Alex thought for a moment. Wolf hadn't moved. Alex could see his shoulders rising and falling as he tried to summon up the courage to go. Ten seconds had passed. Maybe more. The assistant pilot was leaning down, stowing away a piece of equipment. Alex stood up. "Wolf," he said.

Wolf didn't even hear him.

Alex took one last quick look at the assistant pilot, then kicked out with all his strength. His foot slammed into Wolf's backside. He'd put all his strength behind it. Wolf was caught by surprise, his hands coming free as he plunged into the swirling night air.

The assistant pilot turned round and saw Alex. "What are you doing?" he shouted.

"Just stretching my legs," Alex shouted back.

The plane curved in the air and began the journey home.

Mrs Jones was waiting for him when he walked into the hangar. She was sitting at a table, wearing a grey silk jacket and trousers with a black handkerchief flowing out of her top pocket. For a moment she didn't recognize him. Alex was dressed in a flying suit. His hair was damp from the rain. His face was pinched with tiredness and he seemed to have grown older very fast. None of the men had arrived back yet. A truck had been sent to collect them from a field about three kilometres away.

"Alex?" she said.

Alex looked at her but said nothing.

"It was my decision to stop you jumping," she said. "I hope you're not disappointed. I just thought it was too much of a risk. Please. Sit down."

Alex sat down opposite her.

"I have something that might cheer you up," she went on. "I've brought you some toys."

"I'm too old for toys," Alex said.

"Not these toys."

She signalled and a man appeared, walking out of the shadows, carrying a tray of equipment, which he set down on the table. The man was enormously fat. When he sat down, the metal chair disappeared beneath the spread of his buttocks and Alex was surprised it could even take his weight. He was bald, with a black moustache and several chins, each one melting into the next and finally into his neck and shoulders. He wore a pinstriped suit which must have used enough material to make a tent.

"Smithers," he said, nodding at Alex. "Very nice to meet you, old chap."

"What have you got for him?" Mrs Jones demanded.

"I'm afraid we haven't had a great deal of time, Mrs J," Smithers replied. "The challenge was to think what a fourteen-year-old might carry with him – and adapt it." He picked the first object off the tray. A yo-yo. It was slightly larger than normal, made of black plastic. "Let's start with this," Smithers said.

Alex shook his head. He couldn't believe any of this. "Don't tell me!" he exclaimed. "It's some sort of secret weapon..."

"Not exactly. I was told you weren't to have weapons. You're too young."

"So it's not really a hand grenade? Pull the string and run like hell?"

"Certainly not. It's a yo-yo." Smithers pulled out the string, holding it between a podgy finger and thumb. "However, the string is a special sort of nylon. Very advanced. There are thirty metres of it and it can lift weights of up to one hundred kilograms. The actual yo-yo is motorized and clips on to your belt. Very useful for climbing."

"Amazing." Alex was unimpressed.

"And then there's this." Smithers produced a small tube. Alex read the side: ZIT-CLEAN, FOR HEALTHIER SKIN. "Nothing personal," Smithers went on apologetically, "but we thought it was something a boy of your age might use. And it is rather remarkable." He opened the tube and squeezed some of the cream on to his finger. "Completely harmless when you touch it. But bring it into contact with metal and it's quite another story." He wiped his finger, smearing the cream on to the surface of the table. For a moment nothing happened. Then a wisp of acrid smoke twisted upwards in the air, the metal sizzled and a jagged hole appeared. "It'll do that to just about any metal," Smithers explained. "Very useful if you need to break through a lock." He took out a handkerchief and wiped his finger clean.

"Anything else?" Mrs Jones asked.

"Oh yes, Mrs J. You could say this is our *pièce de résistance*." He picked up a brightly coloured box that Alex recognized at once as a Nintendo DS. "What teenager would be complete without one of these?" he asked. "This one comes with four games. And the beauty of it is, each game turns the computer into something quite different."

He showed Alex the first game. "If you insert Nemesis, the computer becomes a fax/photocopier which gives you direct contact with us and vice versa." A second game. "Exocet turns the computer into an X-ray device. It has an audio function too. The headphones are useful for eavesdropping. It's not as powerful as I'd like, but we're working on it. Speed Wars is a bug finder. I suggest you use it the moment you're shown to your room. And finally ... Bomber Boy."

"Do I get to play that one?" Alex asked.

"You can play all four of them. But as the name might suggest, this is actually a smoke bomb. You leave the game cartridge somewhere in a room and press START three times on the console and it will go off. Useful camouflage if you need to escape in a hurry."

"Thank you, Smithers," Mrs Jones said.

"My pleasure, Mrs J." Smithers stood up, his legs straining to take the huge weight. "I'll hope to see you again, Alex. I've never had to equip a boy before. I'm sure I'll be able to think up a whole host of quite delightful ideas."

He waddled off and disappeared through a door which clanged shut behind him.

Mrs Jones turned to Alex. "You leave tomorrow for Port Tallon," she said. "You'll be going under the name of Felix Lester." She handed him a folder. "We've sent the real Felix Lester on holiday in Scotland. You'll find everything you need to know about him in here."

"I'll read it in bed."

"Good." Suddenly she was serious and Alex found himself wondering if she was herself a mother. If so, she could well have a son of his age. She took out a black and white photograph and laid it on the table. It showed a man in a white T-shirt and jeans. He was in his late twenties with blond, close-cropped hair, a smooth face, the body of a dancer. The photograph was slightly blurred. It had been taken from a distance, as if with a hidden camera. "I want you to look at this," she said.

"I'm looking."

"His name is Yassen Gregorovich. He was born in Russia but he now works for many countries. Iraq has employed him. Also Serbia, Libya and China."

"What does he do?" Alex asked, though looking at the cold face with its blank, hooded eyes, he could almost guess.

"He's a contract killer, Alex. We believe he killed Ian Rider."

There was a long pause. Alex stared at the photograph, trying to print it on his mind.

"This photograph was taken six months ago, in Cuba. It may have been a coincidence but Herod Sayle was there at the same time. The two of them might have met. And there is something else." She paused. "Rider used a code in the last message he sent. A single letter. Y."

"Y for Yassen."

"He must have seen Yassen somewhere in Port Tallon. He wanted us to know—"

"Why are you telling me this now?" Alex asked.

"Because if you see him – if Yassen is anywhere near Sayle Enterprises – I want you to contact us at once."

"And then?"

"We'll pull you out. If Yassen finds out you're working for us, he'll kill you too."

Alex smiled. "I'm too young to interest him," he said.

"No." Mrs Jones took the photograph back. "Just remember, Alex Rider, you're never too young to die."

Alex stood up.

"You'll leave tomorrow morning at eight o'clock," Mrs Jones said. "Be careful, Alex. And good luck."

Alex walked across the hangar, his footsteps echoing. Behind him, Mrs Jones unwrapped a peppermint and slipped it into her mouth. Her breath always smelt faintly of mint. As Head of Special Operations, how many men had she sent to their deaths? Ian Rider and maybe dozens more. Perhaps it was easier for her if her breath was sweet.

There was a movement ahead of him and he saw that the parachutists had got back from their jump. They were walking towards him out of the darkness, with Wolf and the other men from K Unit right at the front. Alex tried to step round them but he found Wolf blocking his way.

"You're leaving," Wolf said. Somehow he must have heard that Alex's training was over.

"Yes."

There was a long pause. "What happened on the plane..." he began.

"Forget it, Wolf," Alex said. "Nothing happened. You jumped and I didn't, that's all."

Wolf held out a hand. "I want you to know ... I was wrong about you. I'm sorry I gave you such a hard time. But you're all right. And maybe ... one day it would be good to work with you."

"You never know," Alex said.

They shook.

"Good luck, Cub."

"Goodbye, Wolf."

Alex walked out into the night.

PHYSALIA PHYSALIS

The silver-grey Mercedes SL600 cruised down the motorway, travelling south. Alex was sitting in the front passenger seat, with so much soft leather around him that he could barely hear the 389-horsepower, 6-litre engine that was carrying him towards the Sayle complex near Port Tallon, Cornwall. But at eighty miles per hour, the engine was only idling. Alex could feel the power of the car. One hundred thousand pounds' worth of German engineering. One touch from the thin, unsmiling chauffeur and the Mercedes would leap forward. This was a car that sneered at speed limits.

Alex had been collected that morning from a converted church in Hampstead, north London. This was where Felix Lester lived. When the driver had arrived, Alex had been waiting with his luggage and there'd even been a woman – an MI6 operative – kissing him, telling him to clean his teeth, waving goodbye. As far as the driver was concerned, Alex was Felix. That morning Alex had read through the file and knew that Lester went to a school called St Anthony's, had two sisters and a pet Labrador. His father was an architect. His mother designed jewellery. A happy family – *his* family if anybody asked.

"How far is it to Port Tallon?" he asked.

So far the driver had barely spoken a word. He answered Alex without looking at him. "A few hours. You want some music?"

"Got any John Lennon?" That wasn't his choice. According to the file, Felix Lester liked John Lennon.

"No."

"Forget it. I'll get some sleep."

He needed the sleep. He was still exhausted from the training and wondered how he would explain all the half-healed cuts and bruises if anyone saw under his shirt. Maybe he'd tell them he got bullied at school. He closed his eyes and allowed the leather to suck him into sleep.

It was the feeling of the car slowing down that woke him. He opened his eyes and saw a fishing village, the blue sea beyond, a swathe of rolling green hills and a cloudless sky. It was a picture off a jigsaw puzzle, or perhaps a holiday brochure advertising a forgotten England. Seagulls swooped and cried overhead. An old tug – tangled nets, smoke and flaking paint – pulled into the quay. A few locals, fishermen and their wives, stood around, watching. It was about five o'clock in the afternoon and the village was caught in the silvery, fragile light that comes at the end of a perfect spring day.

"Port Tallon," the driver said. He must have noticed Alex opening his eyes.

"It's pretty."

"Not if you're a fish."

They drove round the edge of the village and back inland, down a lane that twisted between strangely bumpy fields. Alex saw the ruins of buildings, half-crumbling chimneys and rusting metal wheels, and knew that he was looking at an old tin mine. They'd mined tin in Cornwall for three thousand years until one day the tin had run out. Now all that was left were the holes.

A couple of kilometres down the lane a linked metal fence sprang up. It was brand-new, ten metres high, topped with razor wire. Arc lamps on scaffolding towers stood at regular intervals and there were huge signs, red on white. You could have read them from the next county.

SAYLE *Enterprises*
STRICTLY PRIVATE

"Trespassers will be shot," Alex muttered to himself. He remembered what Mrs Jones had told him. *He's more or less got his own private army. He's acting as if he's got something to hide.* Well, that was certainly his own first impression. The whole complex was somehow shocking, alien to the sloping hills and fields.

The car reached the main gate, where there was a security cabin and an electronic barrier. A guard in a blue and grey uniform with **SE** printed on his jacket waved them through. The barrier lifted automatically. And then they were following a long, straight road over a stretch of land that had somehow been hammered flat, with an airstrip on one side and a cluster of four high-tech buildings on the other. The buildings were large, smoked glass and steel, each one joined to the next by a covered walkway. There were two aircraft next to the landing-strip. A helicopter and a small cargo plane. Alex was impressed. The whole complex must have been about five kilometres square. It was quite an operation.

The Mercedes came to a roundabout with a fountain at the centre, swept round it and continued up towards a fantastic, sprawling house. It was Victorian, red brick topped with copper domes and spires that had long ago turned green. There must have been at least sixty windows on the five floors facing the drive. It was a house that just didn't know when to stop.

The Mercedes pulled up at the main entrance and the driver got out. "Follow me."

"What about my luggage?" Alex asked.

"It'll be brought."

Alex and the driver went through the front door and into a hall dominated by a huge canvas – Judgement Day, the end of the world, painted four centuries ago as a swirling mass of doomed souls and demons. There were works of art everywhere. Watercolours and oils, prints, drawings, sculptures in stone and bronze, all crowded together with nowhere for the eye to rest. Alex followed the driver along a carpet so thick that he almost bounced. He was beginning to feel claustrophobic and was relieved when they passed through a door and into a vast room that was practically bare.

"Mr Sayle will be here shortly," the driver said, and left.

Alex looked around him. This was a modern room with a curving steel desk near the centre, carefully positioned halogen lights and a spiral staircase leading down from a perfect circle cut in the ceiling high above. One entire wall consisted of a single sheet of glass and, walking over to it, Alex realized that he was looking at a gigantic aquarium. The sheer size of the thing drew him towards it. It was hard to imagine how many thousands of litres of water the glass held back, but he was surprised to see that the tank was empty. There were no fish, although it was big enough to hold a shark.

And then something moved in the turquoise shadows and Alex gasped with a mixture of horror and wonderment as the biggest jellyfish he had ever seen drifted into view. The main body of the creature was a shimmering, pulsating mass of white and mauve, shaped roughly like a cone. Beneath it, a mass of tentacles covered with circular stingers twisted in the water, at least ten metres long. As the jellyfish moved, or drifted in an artificial current, its tentacles writhed against the glass so that it looked almost as if it was trying to break out. It was the single most awesome and repulsive thing Alex had ever seen.

"*Physalia physalis.*" The voice came from behind him and Alex twisted round to see a man coming down the last of the stairs.

Herod Sayle was short. He was so short that Alex's first impression was that he was looking at a reflection that had somehow been distorted. In his immaculate and expensive black suit, with gold signet-ring and brightly polished black shoes, he looked like a scaled-down model of a multi-millionaire businessman. His skin was very dark, so that his teeth flashed when he smiled. He had a round, bald head and very horrible eyes. The grey irises were too small, completely surrounded by white. Alex was reminded of tadpoles before they hatch. When Sayle stood next to him, the eyes were almost at the same level as his and held less warmth than the jellyfish.

"The Portuguese man-o'-war," Sayle continued. He had a heavy accent brought with him from the Beirut marketplace. "It's beautiful, don't you think?"

"I wouldn't keep one as a pet," Alex said.

"I came upon this one when I was diving in the South China Sea." Sayle gestured at a glass display case and Alex noticed three harpoon guns and a collection of knives resting in velvet slots. "I love to kill fish," Sayle went on. "But when I saw this specimen of *Physalia physalis*, I knew I had to capture it and keep it. You see, it reminds me of myself."

"It's ninety-nine per cent water. It has no brain, no guts and no anus." Alex had dredged up the facts from somewhere and spoken them before he knew what he was doing.

Sayle glanced at him, then turned back to the creature hovering over him in its tank. "It's an outsider," he said. "It drifts on its own, ignored by the other fish. It is silent and yet it demands respect. You see the nematocysts, Mr Lester? The stinging cells? If you were to find yourself wrapped in those, it would be an exquisite death."

"Call me Alex," Alex said.

He'd meant to say Felix, but somehow it had slipped out. It was the most stupid, the most amateurish mistake he could have made. But he had been thrown by the way Sayle had appeared and by the slow, hypnotic dance of the jellyfish.

The grey eyes squirmed. "I thought your name was Felix."

"My friends call me Alex."

"Why?"

"After Alex Ferguson. I'm a big fan of Manchester United and he was the best manager they ever had." It was the first thing Alex could think of. But he'd seen a football poster in Felix Lester's bedroom and knew that at least he'd chosen the right team.

Sayle smiled. "That's most amusing. Alex it shall be. And I hope we will be friends, Alex. You are a very lucky boy. You won the competition and you are going to be the first teenager to try out my Stormbreaker. But this is also lucky, I think, for me. I want to know what you think of it. I want you to tell me what you like ... what you don't." The eyes dipped away and suddenly he was business-like. "We have only three days until the launch," he said. "We'd better get a *bliddy* move on, as my father used to say. I'll have my man take you to your room and tomorrow morning, first thing, you must get to work. There's a maths program you should try ... also languages. All the software was developed here at Sayle Enterprises. Of course, we've talked to children. We've gone to teachers, to education experts. But you, my dear ... Alex. You will be worth more to me than all of them put together."

As he had talked, Sayle had become more and

more animated, carried away by his own enthusiasm. He had become a completely different man. Alex had to admit that he'd taken an immediate dislike to Herod Sayle. No wonder Blunt and the people at MI6 mistrusted him! But now he was forced to think again. He was standing opposite one of the richest men in England, a man who had decided, out of the goodness of his heart, to give a huge gift to British schools. Just because he was small and slimy, that didn't necessarily make him an enemy. Perhaps Blunt was wrong after all.

"Ah! Here's my man now," Sayle said. "And about *bliddy* time!"

The door had opened and a man had come in, dressed in the black suit and tails of an old-fashioned butler. He was as tall and thin as his master was short and round, with a thatch of ginger hair above a face so pale it was almost paper white. From a distance it had looked as if he was smiling, but as he drew closer Alex gasped. The man had two horrendous scars, one on each side of his mouth, twisting up all the way to his ears. It was as if someone had attempted to cut his face in half. The scars were a gruesome shade of mauve. There were smaller, fainter scars where his cheeks had once been stitched.

"This is Mr Grin," Sayle said. "He changed his name after his accident."

"Accident?" Alex found it hard not to stare at the terrible wounds.

"Mr Grin used to work in a circus. It was a novelty knife-throwing act. For the climax he used to catch a spinning knife between his teeth, but then one night his elderly mother came to see the show. She waved to him from the front row and he got his timing wrong. He's worked for me for a dozen years now and although his appearance may be displeasing, he is loyal and efficient. Don't try to talk with him, by the way. He has no tongue."

"Eeeurgh!" Mr Grin said.

"Nice to meet you," Alex muttered.

"Take him to the blue room," Sayle commanded. He turned to Alex. "You're fortunate that one of our nicest rooms has come up free – here, in the house. We had a security man staying there. But he left us quite suddenly."

"Oh? Why was that?" Alex asked casually.

"I have no idea. One moment he was here, the next he was gone." Sayle smiled again. "I hope you won't do the same, Alex."

"Ri ... wurgh!" Mr Grin gestured at the door and, leaving Herod Sayle standing in front of his huge captive, Alex left the room.

He was led along a passage past more works of art, up a staircase and then along a wide corridor with thick wood-panelled doors and chandeliers. Alex assumed that the main house was used for entertaining. Sayle himself must live here. But the computers would be constructed in the modern buildings he had seen opposite the airstrip. Presumably he would be taken there tomorrow.

His room was at the far end. It was a large room with a four-poster bed and a window looking out on to the fountain. Darkness had fallen and the water, cascading ten metres through the air over a semi-naked statue that looked remarkably like Herod Sayle, was eerily illuminated by a dozen concealed lights. Next to the window was a table with an evening meal already laid out for him: ham, cheese, salad. His bag was lying on the bed.

He went over to it – a Nike sports bag – and examined it. When he had closed it up, he had inserted three hairs into the zip, trapping them in the metal teeth. They were no longer there. Alex opened the bag and went through it. Everything was exactly as it had been when he had packed, but he was certain that the sports bag had been expertly and methodically searched.

He took out the Nintendo DS, inserted the Speed Wars cartridge and pressed the START button three times. At once the top screen lit up with a green rectangle, the same shape as the room. He lifted the Nintendo up and swung it around him, following the line of the walls. A red flashing dot suddenly appeared on the top screen. He walked forward, holding the Nintendo in front of him. The dot flashed faster, more intensely. He had reached a picture, hanging next to the bathroom, a squiggle of colours that looked suspiciously like a Picasso. He put the Nintendo down and carefully lifted the canvas off the wall. The bug was taped behind it, a black disc about the size of a ten pence piece. Alex looked at it for a minute, wondering why it was there. Security? Or was Sayle such a control freak that he had to know what his guests were doing every minute of the day and night?

Alex put the picture back. There was only one bug in the room. The bathroom was clean.

He ate his dinner, showered and got ready for bed. As he passed the window, he noticed activity in the grounds near the fountain. There were lights shining out of the modern buildings. Three men, all dressed in white overalls, were driving towards the house in an open-top Jeep. Two more men walked past. These were security guards, dressed in the same uniform as the man at the gate. They were both carrying semi-automatic machine-guns. Not just a private army, but a well-armed one.

He got into bed. The last person who had slept here had been his uncle, Ian Rider. Had he seen something, looking out of the window? Had he heard something? What could have happened that meant he had to die?

Sleep took a long time coming to the dead man's bed.

LOOKING FOR TROUBLE

Alex saw it the moment he opened his eyes. It would have been obvious to anyone who slept in the bed, but of course nobody had slept there since Ian Rider had been killed. It was a triangle of white slipped into a fold in the canopy above the four-poster bed. You had to be lying on your back to see it – like Alex was now.

It was out of his reach. He had to balance a chair on the mattress and then stand on the chair to reach it. Wobbling, almost falling, he finally managed to trap it between his fingers and pull it out.

In fact it was a square of paper, folded twice. Someone had drawn on it, a strange design with what looked like a reference number beneath it.

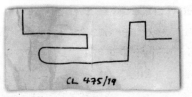

CL 475/19

There wasn't very much of it, but Alex recognized Ian Rider's handwriting. But what did it mean? He pulled on some clothes, went over to the table and took out a sheet of plain paper. Quickly, he wrote a brief message in block capitals.

FOUND THIS IN IAN RIDER'S ROOM. CAN YOU MAKE ANY SENSE OF IT?

Then he found his Nintendo DS, inserted the Nemesis cartridge into the back, turned it on and passed the bottom screen over the two sheets of paper, scanning first his message and then the design. In a matter of micro-seconds the image would appear on the screen of Mrs Jones's computer in London along with the time and the location from which it had been sent. Maybe she could work it out. She was, after all, meant to work for Intelligence.

Finally, Alex turned off the Nintendo then removed the back and hid the folded paper in the battery compartment. The diagram had to be important. Ian Rider had hidden it. Maybe it was what had cost him his life.

There was a knock at the door. Alex went over and opened it. Mr Grin was standing outside, still wearing his butler's uniform.

"Good morning," Alex said.

"Geurgh!" Mr Grin gestured and Alex followed him back down the corridor and out of the house. He felt relieved to be out in the air, away from all the artwork. As they paused in front of the fountain there was a sudden roar and a propeller-driven cargo plane dipped down over the roof of the house and landed on the runway.

"If gring gly," Mr Grin explained.

"Just as I thought," Alex said.

They reached the first of the modern buildings and Mr Grin pressed his hand against a glass plate next to the door. There was a green glow as his fingerprints were read, and a moment later the door slid soundlessly open.

Everything was different on the other side of the door. From the art and elegance of the main house, Alex could have stepped into the next century. Long white corridors with metallic floors. Halogen lights. The unnatural chill of air-conditioning. Another world.

A woman was waiting for them, broad-shouldered and severe, her blonde hair twisted into the tightest of buns. She had a strangely blank, moon-shaped face, wire-framed spectacles and no make-up apart from a smear of yellow lipstick. She wore a white coat with a name tag pinned to the top pocket. It read: VOLE.

"You must be Felix," she said. "Or is it now, I understand, Alex? Yes! Allow me to introduce myself. I am Fräulein Vole." She had a thick German accent. "You may call me Nadia." She glanced at Mr Grin. "I will take him from here."

Mr Grin nodded and left the building.

"Do you have a mobile?" Vole asked holding out her hand.

"Sure." Alex handed it across.

"I am afraid I will be keeping it until the end of your visit. A security measure, you understand." She slipped it into her pocket.

Alex was sorry to see it go. Not being allowed a phone at school was bad enough but here, in the middle of Sayle's compound, he felt lost without it. But it was too late. Nadia Vole had already set off, talking as she went. "We have four blocks here. Block A where we are now, is Administration and Recreation. Block B is Software Development. Block C is Research and Storage. Block D is where the main Stormbreaker assembly line is found."

"Where's breakfast?" Alex asked.

"You have not eaten? I will send you a sandwich. Herr Sayle is very keen for you to begin at once with the experience."

She walked like a soldier – back straight, her feet, in black leather shoes, rapping against the floor. Alex followed her through a door and into a bare, square room with a chair and a desk and, on the desk, the first actual Stormbreaker he had ever seen.

It was a beautiful machine. The iMac might have been the first computer with a real sense of design, but the Stormbreaker had far surpassed it. It was black apart from the white lightning bolt down one side – and the screen could have been a porthole into outer space. Alex sat behind the desk and turned it on. The computer booted itself instantly. A fork of animated lightning sliced across the screen, there was a swirl of clouds, and then in burning red the letters **SE**, the logo of Sayle Enterprises, formed itself. Seconds later, the desktop appeared, with icons for maths, science, French – every subject – ready to be accessed. Even in those brief seconds, Alex could feel the speed and the power of the computer. And Herod Sayle was going to put one in every school in the country! He had to admire the man. It was an incredible gift.

"I leave you here," Fräulein Vole said. "It is better for you, I think, to explore the Stormbreaker on your own. Tonight you will have dinner with Herr Sayle and you will tell him your feeling."

"Yeah – I'll tell him my feeling."

"I will have the sandwich sent in to you. But I must ask you to please not leave the room. There is, you understand, the security."

"Whatever you say, Mrs Vole," Alex said.

The woman left. Alex opened one of the programs and for the next three hours lost himself in the state-of-the-art software of the Stormbreaker. Even when his sandwich arrived, he ignored it, letting it curl on the plate. He would never have said that school-work was fun, but he had to admit that the computer made it lively. The history program brought the battle of Port Stanley to life with music and video clips. How to extract oxygen from water? The science program did it in front of his eyes. The Stormbreaker even managed to make geometry almost bearable, which was more than Mr Donovan at Brookland had ever done.

The next time Alex looked at his watch it was

one o'clock. He had been in the room for over four hours. He stretched and stood up. Nadia Vole had told him not to leave, but if there were any secrets to be found at Sayle Enterprises, he wasn't going to find them here. He walked over to the door and was surprised to find that it opened as he approached. He went out into the corridor. There was nobody in sight. Time to move.

Block A was Administration and Recreation. Alex passed a number of offices, then a blank, white-tiled cafeteria. There were about forty men and women, all in white coats and identity tags, sitting and talking animatedly over their lunches. He had chosen a good time. Nobody passed him as he continued through a Plexiglas walkway into Block B. There were computer screens everywhere, glowing in cramped offices piled high with papers and printouts. Software Development. Through to Block C – Research – past a library with endless shelves of books and hard drives. Alex ducked in behind a shelf as two technicians walked past, talking together. He was out of bounds, on his own, snooping around without any idea of what he was looking for. Trouble, probably. What else could there be to find?

He walked softly, casually, down the corridor, heading for the last block. A murmur of voices reached him and he quickly stepped into an alcove, squatting down beside a drinking fountain as two men and a woman walked past, all wearing white coats, arguing about Web servers. Overhead, he noticed a security camera swivelling towards him. In another five seconds it would be on him, but he still had to wait until the three technicians had gone before he could sprint forward, just ahead of the wide-angle lens.

Had it seen him? Alex couldn't be sure. But he did know one thing: he was running out of time. Maybe the Vole woman would have checked up on him already. Maybe someone would have brought lunch to the empty room. If he was going to find anything, it would have to be soon...

He started along the glass passage that joined Blocks C and D, and here at last there was something different. The corridor was split in half, with a metal staircase leading down into what must have been some sort of basement. And although every building and every door he had seen so far had been labelled, this staircase was blank. The light stopped about halfway down. It was almost as if the stairs were trying not to get themselves noticed.

The clang of feet on metal. Alex shrank back and a moment later Mr Grin appeared, rising out of the floor like a vampire on a bad day. As the sun hit his dead, white face, his scars twitched and he blinked several times before walking off into Block D.

What had he been doing? Where did the stairs go? Alex hurried down them. It was like stepping into a morgue. The air-conditioning was so strong that he could feel it on his forehead and on the palms of his hands, fast-freezing his sweat.

He stopped at the bottom of the stairs. He was in another long passageway, stretching back under the complex, the way he had come. It led to a single metal door. But there was something very strange. The walls of the passage were unfinished; dark brown rock with streaks of what looked like zinc or some other metal. The floor was also rough, and the way was lit by old-fashioned bulbs hanging on wires. It all reminded him of something ... something he had seen very recently. But he couldn't remember what.

Somehow Alex knew that the door at the end of the passage would be locked. It looked as if it had been locked for ever. Like the stairs, it was not labelled. And somehow it seemed too small to be important. But Mr Grin had just come up the stairs. There was only one place he could have come from and that was the other side. The door had to lead somewhere!

He reached it and tried the handle. It wouldn't move. He pressed his ear against the metal and listened. Nothing, unless ... was he imagining it? ... a sort of throbbing. A pump or something like it. Alex would have given anything to see through the metal – and suddenly he realized that he could. The Nintendo was in his pocket. He took it out, inserted the Exocet cartridge, turned it on and held it flat against the door.

The top screen flickered into life; a tiny window through the metal door. Alex was looking into a large room. There was something tall and barrel-shaped in the middle of it. And there were people. Ghost-like, mere smudges on the screen, they were moving back and forth. Some of them were carrying objects – flat and rectangular. Trays of some sort? There seemed to be a desk to one side, piled with apparatus that he couldn't make out. Alex pressed the B button, trying to zoom in. But the room was too big. Everything was too far away.

He fumbled in his pocket and took out the earphones. Still holding the Nintendo against the door, he pressed the wire into the socket and slipped the earphones over his head. If he couldn't see, at least he might be able to hear – and sure enough the voices came through, faint and disconnected, but audible through the powerful speaker system built into the machine.

"...in place. We have twenty-four hours."

"It's not enough."

"It's all we have. They come in tonight. At 0200."

Alex didn't recognize any of the voices. Amplified by the tiny machine, they sounded like a phone call from abroad on a very bad line.

"...Grin ... overseeing the delivery."

"It's still not enough time."

And then they were gone. Alex tried to piece together what he had heard. Something was being delivered. Two hours after midnight. Mr Grin was arranging the delivery.

But what? Why?

He had just turned off the Nintendo and put it back into his pocket when he heard behind him the squeak of a shoe that told him he was no longer alone. He turned round and found himself facing Nadia Vole. Alex realized that she had tried to sneak up on him. She had known he was down here.

"What are you doing, Alex?" she asked. Her voice was poisoned honey.

"Nothing," Alex said.

"I asked you to stay in the computer room."

"Yes. But I'd been there all morning. I needed a break."

"And you came down here?"

"I saw the stairs. I thought they might lead to the toilet."

There was a long silence. Behind him, Alex could still hear – or feel – the throbbing from the secret room. Then the woman nodded as if she had decided to accept his story. "There is nothing down here," she said. "This door leads only to the generator room. Please..." She gestured. "I will take you back to the main house, yes? And later you must prepare for the dinner with Herr Sayle. He wishes to know your first impressions of the Stormbreaker."

Alex walked past her and back towards the stairs. He was certain of two things. The first was that Nadia Vole was lying. This was no generator room. She was hiding something. And she hadn't believed him either. One of the cameras must have spotted him and she had been sent to find him. So she knew that he was lying to her.

Not a good start.

Alex reached the staircase and climbed up into the light, feeling the woman's eyes, like daggers, stabbing into his back.

NIGHT VISITORS

Herod Sayle was playing snooker when Alex was shown back into the room with the jellyfish. It was hard to say quite where the heavy wooden snooker table had come from, and Alex couldn't avoid thinking that the little man looked slightly ridiculous, almost lost at the far end of the green baize. Mr Grin was with him, carrying a footstool which Sayle stood on for each shot. Otherwise he would barely have been able to reach over the edge.

"Ah ... good evening, Felix. Or, of course, I mean Alex!" Sayle exclaimed. "Do you play snooker?"

"Occasionally."

"How would you like to play against me? There are only two reds left – then the colours. But I'm willing to bet that you don't manage to score a single point."

"How much?"

"Ha ha!" Sayle laughed. "Suppose I was to bet you ten pounds a point?"

"As much as that?" Alex looked surprised.

"To a man like myself, ten pounds is nothing. Nothing! Why, I could quite happily bet you a hundred pounds a point!"

"Then why don't you?" The words were softly spoken but they were still a direct challenge. Sayle gazed thoughtfully at Alex. "Very well," he said. "A hundred pounds a point. Why not? I like a gamble. My father was a gambling man."

"I thought he was a hairdresser."

"Who told you that?"

Silently, Alex cursed himself. Why was he never more careful when he was with this man? "I read it in a paper," he said. "My dad got me some stuff to read about you when I won the competition."

"A hundred pounds a point, then. But don't expect to get rich." Sayle hit the white, sending one of the reds straight into the middle pocket. The jellyfish floated past as if watching the game from its tank. Mr Grin picked up the footstool and moved it round the table. Sayle laughed briefly and followed the butler round, already sizing up the next shot, a fairly tricky black into the corner. "So what does your father do?" he asked.

"He's an architect," Alex said.

"Oh yes? What has he designed?" The question was casual, but Alex wondered if he was being tested.

"He's been working on an office in Soho," Alex said. "Before that he did an art gallery in Aberdeen."

"Yes." Sayle climbed on to the footstool and aimed. The black missed the corner pocket by a fraction of a millimetre, spinning back into the centre. Sayle frowned. "That was your *bliddy* fault," he snapped at Mr Grin.

"Warg?"

"Your shadow was on the table. Never mind, never mind!" He turned to Alex. "You've been unlucky. None of the balls will go in. You won't make any money this time."

Alex pulled a cue out of the rack and glanced at the table. Sayle was right. The last red was too close to the cushion. But in snooker there are other ways to win points, as Alex knew only too well. It was one of the many games he had played with Ian Rider. The two of them had even belonged to a club in Chelsea and Alex had represented the junior team. This was something he hadn't mentioned to Sayle. He carefully aimed at the red, then hit. Perfect.

"Nowhere near!" Sayle was back at the table before the balls had even stopped rolling. But he had spoken too soon. He stared as the white ball hit the cushion and rolled behind the pink. He'd been snookered. For about twenty seconds he measured up the angles, breathing through his nose. "You've had a bit of *bliddy* luck!" he said. "You seem to have accidentally snookered me. Now, let me see..." He concentrated, then hit the white, trying to curve it round the pink. But once again he was out by about a millimetre. There was an audible click as it touched the pink.

"Foul shot," Alex said. "Six points to me. Does that mean I get six hundred pounds?"

"What?"

"The foul is worth six points to me. At a hundred pounds a point—"

"Yes, yes, yes!" Saliva flecked Sayle's lips. He was staring at the table as if he couldn't believe what had happened.

His shot had exposed the red ball. It was an easy shot into the top corner and Alex took it without hesitating. "And another hundred makes seven hundred," he said. He moved down the table, brushing past Mr Grin. Quickly he judged the angles. Yes...

He got a perfect kiss on the black, sending it into the corner with the white spinning back for a good angle on the yellow. One thousand four hundred pounds plus another two hundred when he dropped the yellow immediately afterwards. Sayle could only watch in disbelief as Alex pocketed the green, the brown, the blue and the pink in that order and then, down the full length of the table, the black.

"I make that four thousand, one hundred pounds," Alex said. He put down the cue. "Thank you very much."

Sayle's face had gone the colour of the last ball. "Four thousand...! I wouldn't have gambled if I'd known you were this *bliddy* good," he said. He went over to the wall and pressed a button. Part of the floor slid back and the entire pool-table disappeared into it, carried down by a hydraulic lift. When the floor slid back, there was no sign that it had ever been there. It was a neat trick. The toy of a man with money to burn.

But Sayle was no longer in the mood for games. He threw his billiard-cue over to Mr Grin, hurling it almost like a javelin. The butler's hand flicked out and caught it. "Let's eat," Sayle said.

*   *   *

The two of them sat at opposite ends of a long glass table in the room next door while Mr Grin served smoked salmon, then some sort of stew. Alex drank water. Sayle, who had cheered up once again, had a glass of vintage red wine.

"You spent some time with the Stormbreaker today?" he asked.

"Yes."

"And...?"

"It's great," Alex said, and meant it. He still found it hard to believe that this ridiculous man could have created anything so sleek and powerful.

"So which programs did you use?"

"History. Science. Maths. It's hard to believe, but I actually enjoyed them!"

"Do you have any criticisms?"

Alex thought for a moment. "I was surprised it didn't have 3D acceleration."

"The Stormbreaker is not intended for games."

"Did you consider a headset and integrated microphone?"

"No." Sayle nodded. "It's a good idea. I'm sorry you've only come here for such a short time, Alex. Tomorrow we'll have to get you on to the Internet. The Stormbreakers are all connected to a master network. That's controlled from here. It means they have free twenty-four-hour access."

"That's cool."

"It's more than cool." Sayle's eyes were far away, the grey irises small, dancing. "Tomorrow we start shipping the computers out," he said. "They'll go by plane, by lorry and by boat. It will take just one day for them to reach every point of the country. And the day after, at twelve o'clock noon exactly, the Prime Minister will honour me by pressing the START button which will bring every one of my Stormbreakers on-line. At that moment, all the schools will be united. Think of it, Alex! Thousands of schoolchildren – hundreds of thousands – sitting in front of the screens, suddenly together. North, south, east and west. One school. One family. And then they will know me for what I am!"

He picked up his glass and emptied it. "How is the goat?" he asked.

"I'm sorry?"

"The stew. It's goat meat with spinach and lentils. It was a recipe of my mother's."

"She must have been an unusual woman."

Herod Sayle held out his glass and Mr Grin refilled it. Sayle was gazing at Alex curiously. "You know," he said. "I have a strange feeling that you and I have met before."

"I don't think so—"

"But yes. Your face is familiar to me. Mr Grin? What do you think?"

The butler stood back with the wine. His dead, white head twisted round to look at Alex. "Eeeg Raargh!" he said.

"Yes, of course. You're right!"

"Eeeg Raargh?" Alex asked.

"Ian Rider. The security man I mentioned. You look a lot like him. Quite a coincidence, don't you think?"

"I don't know. I never met him." Alex could feel the danger getting closer. "You told me he left suddenly."

"Yes. He was sent here to keep an eye on things, but if you ask me he was never any *bliddy* good. Spent half his time in the village. In the port, the post office, the library. When he wasn't snooping around here, that is. Of course, that's something else you have in common. I understand Fräulein Vole found you today..." Sayle's pupils crawled to the front of his eyes, trying to get closer to Alex. "You were off limits."

"I got a bit lost." Alex shrugged, trying to make light of it.

"Well, I hope you don't go wandering again tonight. Security is very tight at the moment and, as you may have noticed, my men are all armed."

"I didn't think that was legal in Britain."

"We have a special licence. At any rate, Alex, I would advise you to go straight to your room after dinner. And stay there. I would be inconsolable if you were accidentally shot and killed in the darkness. Although it would, of course, save me four thousand pounds."

"Actually, I think you've forgotten the cheque."

"You'll have it tomorrow. Maybe we can have dinner together. Mr Grin will be serving up one of my grandmother's recipes."

"More goat?"

"Dog."

"You obviously had a family that loved animals."

"Only the edible ones." Sayle smiled. "And now I must wish you goodnight."

At one-thirty in the morning, Alex's eyes blinked open and he was instantly awake.

He slipped out of bed and dressed quickly in his darkest clothes, then left the room. He was half-surprised that the door was unlocked and the corridors seemed to be unmonitored. But this was, after all, Sayle's private house and any security would have been designed to stop people coming in, not leaving.

Sayle had warned him not to leave the house. But the voices behind the metal door had spoken of something arriving at two o'clock. Alex had to know what it was.

He found his way into the kitchen and tiptoed past a stretch of gleaming silver surfaces and an oversized American fridge. Let sleeping dogs lie, he thought to himself, remembering what was being served for tomorrow's dinner. There was a side door, fortunately with the key still in the lock. Alex turned it and let himself out. As a last-minute precaution he locked the door and kept the key. Now at least he had a way back in.

It was a soft, grey night with a half-moon forming a perfect D in the sky. D for what, Alex wondered. Danger? Discovery? Or disaster? Only time would tell. He took two steps forward, then froze as a searchlight rolled past, centimetres away, directed from a tower he hadn't even seen. At the same time he became aware of voices, and two guards walked slowly across the garden, patrolling the back of the house. They were both armed and Alex remembered what Sayle had said. An accidental shooting would save him four thousand pounds. And given the importance of the Stormbreakers, would anyone care just how accidental the shooting might have been?

He waited until the men had gone, then took the opposite direction, running along the side of the house, ducking under the windows. He reached the corner and looked round. In the distance, the airstrip was lit up and there were figures – more guards and technicians – everywhere. One man he recognized, walking past the fountain towards a waiting truck. He was tall and gangly, silhouetted against the lights, a black cut-out. But Alex would have known Mr Grin anywhere. *They come in tonight. At 0200.* Night visitors. And Mr Grin was on his way to meet them.

The butler had almost reached the truck and Alex knew that if he waited any longer he would be too late. Throwing caution to the wind, he left the cover of the house and ran out into the open, trying to stay low and hoping his dark clothes would keep him invisible. He was only fifty metres from the truck when Mr Grin suddenly stopped and turned round as if he had sensed there was someone there. There was nowhere for Alex to hide. He did the only thing he could, and threw himself flat on the ground, burying his face in the grass. He counted slowly to five, then looked up. Mr Grin was turning once again. A second figure had appeared ... Nadia Vole. It seemed she would be driving. She muttered something as she climbed into the front. Mr Grin grunted and nodded.

By the time Mr Grin had walked round to the passenger door, Alex was once again up and running. He reached the back of the truck just as it began to move. It was similar to trucks he had seen at the SAS camp. It could have been army surplus. The back was tall and square, covered with tarpaulin. Alex clambered on to the moving tailgate and threw himself in. He was only just in time. Even as he hit the floor, a car started up behind him, flooding the back of the truck with its headlamps. If he had waited even a few seconds more, he would have been seen.

In all, a convoy of five vehicles left Sayle Enterprises. The truck Alex was in was the last but one. As well as Mr Grin and Nadia Vole, at least a dozen uniformed guards were making the journey. But to where? Alex didn't dare look out the back, not with a car right behind him. He felt the truck slow down as they reached the main gate and then they were out on the main road, driving rapidly uphill, away from the village.

Alex felt the journey without seeing it. He was thrown across the metal floor as they sped round hairpin bends, and he only knew they had left the main road when he suddenly found himself being bounced up and down. The truck was moving more slowly. He sensed they were going downhill, following a rough track. And now he could hear something, even over the noise of the engine. Waves. They had come down to the sea.

The truck stopped. There was the opening and slamming of car doors, the scrunch of boots on rocks, low voices talking. Alex crouched down, afraid that one of the guards would throw back the tarpaulin and discover him, but the voices faded and he found himself once again alone. Cautiously, he slipped out the back. He was right. The convoy had parked on a deserted beach. Looking back, he could see a track leading down from the road which twisted up over the cliffs. Mr Grin and the others had gathered beside an old stone jetty that stretched out into the black water. He was carrying a torch. Alex saw him swing it in an arc.

Growing ever more curious, Alex crept forward and found a hiding-place behind a cluster of boulders. It seemed they were waiting for a boat. He looked at his watch. It was exactly two o'clock. He almost wanted to laugh. Give the men flintlock pistols and horses and they could have come straight out of a children's book. Smuggling on the Cornish coast. Could that be what this was all about? Cocaine or marijuana coming in from the Continent? Why else would they be here in the middle of the night?

The question was answered a few seconds later. Alex stared, unable to believe quite what he was seeing.

A submarine. It had emerged from the sea with the speed and impossibility of a huge stage illusion. One moment there was nothing and then it was there in front of him, ploughing through the sea towards the jetty, its engine making no sound, water streaking off its silver casing and churning white behind it. The submarine had no markings, but Alex thought he recognized the shape of the diving plane slashing horizontally through the conning tower and the shark's tail rudder at the back. A Chinese Han Class 404 SSN? Nuclear-powered. Armed, also, with nuclear weapons.

But what was it doing here, off the coast of Cornwall? What was going on?

The tower opened and a man climbed out, stretching himself in the cold morning air. Even without the half-moon, Alex would have recognized the sleek, dancer's body and the close-cropped hair of the man whose photograph he had seen only a few days before. It was Yassen Gregorovich. The contract killer. The man who had murdered Ian Rider. He was dressed in grey overalls. He was smiling.

Yassen Gregorovich had supposedly met Sayle in Cuba. Now here he was in Cornwall. So the two of them *were* working together. But why? Why would the Stormbreaker project need a man like him?

Nadia Vole walked to the end of the jetty and Yassen climbed down to join her. They spoke for a few minutes, but even assuming they were speaking in English, there was no chance of their being overheard. Meanwhile, the guards from Sayle Enterprises had formed a line stretching back almost to the point where the vehicles were parked. Yassen gave an order and, as Alex watched from behind the rocks, a large metallic silver box with a vacuum seal appeared, held by unseen hands, at the top of the submarine's tower. Yassen himself passed it down to the first of the guards, who then passed it back up the line. About forty more boxes followed, one after another. It took almost an hour to unload the submarine. The men handled the boxes carefully. They didn't want to break whatever was inside.

By three o'clock they were almost finished. The boxes were now being packed into the back of the truck that Alex had vacated. And that was when it happened.

One of the men standing on the jetty dropped one of the boxes. He managed to catch it again at the last minute, but even so, it banged down heavily on the stone surface. Everyone stopped. Instantly. It was as if a switch had been thrown, and Alex could almost feel the raw fear in the air.

Yassen was the first to recover. He darted forward along the jetty, moving like a cat, his feet making no sound. He reached the box and ran his hands over it, checking the seal, then nodded slowly. The metal wasn't even dented.

With everyone else so still, Alex heard the exchange that followed.

"It's OK. I'm sorry," the guard said. "It's not damaged and I won't do that again."

"No. You won't," Yassen agreed, and shot him.

The bullet spat out of his hand, red in the darkness. It hit the man in the chest, propelling him backwards in an awkward cartwheel. The man fell into the sea. For a few seconds he looked up at the moon as if trying to admire it one last time. Then the black water folded over him.

It took them another twenty minutes to load

the truck. Yassen got into the front with Nadia Vole. Mr Grin went in one of the cars.

Alex had to time his return carefully. As the truck picked up speed, rumbling back up towards the road, he left the cover of the rocks, ran forward and pulled himself in. There was hardly any room, but he managed to find a hole and squeeze himself into it. He ran a hand over one of the boxes. It was about the size of a tea chest, unmarked, and cold to touch. He tried to find a way to open it, but it was locked in a way he didn't understand.

He looked back out of the truck. The beach and the jetty were already far below them. The submarine was pulling out to sea. One moment it was there, sleek and silver, gliding through the water. Then it had sunk below the surface, disappearing as quickly as a bad dream.

DEATH IN THE LONG GRASS

Alex was woken up by an indignant Nadia Vole knocking at his door. He had overslept.

"This morning it is your last opportunity to experience the Stormbreaker," she said.

"Right," Alex said.

"This afternoon we begin to send the computers out to the schools. Herr Sayle has suggested that you take the afternoon for leisure. A walk perhaps into Port Tallon? There is a footpath that goes through the fields and then by the sea. You will do that, yes?"

"Yes, I'd like that."

"Good. And now I leave you to put on some clothing. I will come back for you in ... *zehn minuten*."

Alex splashed cold water on his face before

getting dressed. It had been four o'clock by the time he had got back to his room and he was still tired. His night expedition hadn't been quite the success he'd hoped. He had seen so much – the submarine, the silver boxes, the death of the guard who had dared to drop one – and yet in the end he still hadn't learned anything.

Was Yassen Gregorovich working for Herod Sayle? He had no proof that Sayle knew he was here. And what about the boxes? They could have contained packed lunches for the staff of Sayle Enterprises for all he knew. Except that you didn't kill a man for dropping a packed lunch.

Today was 31st March. As Vole had said, the computers were on their way out. There was only one day to go until the ceremony at the Science Museum. But Alex had nothing to report and the one piece of information that he had sent – Ian Rider's diagram – had also drawn a blank. There had been a reply waiting for him on the bottom screen of his Nintendo when he turned it on before going to bed.

UNABLE TO RECOGNIZE DIAGRAM OR LETTERS/NUMBERS. POSSIBLE MAP REFERENCE BUT UNABLE TO SOURCE MAP. PLEASE TRANSMIT FURTHER OBSERVATIONS.

Alex had thought of transmitting the fact that he had actually sighted Yassen Gregorovich. But he had decided against it. If Yassen was there, Mrs Jones had promised to pull him out. And suddenly Alex wanted to see this through to the end. Something was going on at Sayle Enterprises. That much was obvious. And he'd never forgive himself if he didn't find out what it was.

Nadia Vole came back for him as promised and he spent the next three hours toying with the Stormbreaker. This time he enjoyed himself less. And this time, he noticed when he went to the door, a guard had been posted in the corridor outside. It seemed that Sayle Enterprises wasn't taking any more chances where he was concerned.

One o'clock arrived and at last the guard released him from the room and escorted him as far as the main gate. It was a glorious afternoon, the sun shining as he walked out on to the road. He took a last look back. Mr Grin had just come out of one of the buildings and was standing some distance away, talking into a mobile phone. There was something unnerving about the sight. Why should he be making a telephone call now? And who could possibly understand a word he said?

It was only once he'd left the plant that Alex was able to relax. Away from the fences, the armed guards and the strange sense of threat that pervaded Sayle Enterprises, it was as if he was breathing fresh air for the first time in days. The Cornish countryside was beautiful, the rolling hills a lush green, dotted with wild flowers.

Alex found the footpath sign and turned off the road. He had worked out that Port Tallon was a couple of miles away, a walk of less than an hour if the route wasn't too hilly. In fact, the path climbed upwards quite steeply almost at once, and suddenly Alex found himself perched over a clear, blue and sparkling English Channel, following a track that zigzagged precariously along the edge of a cliff. To one side of him fields stretched into the distance, their long grass bending in the breeze. To the other there was a fall of at least fifty metres to the rocks and water below. Port Tallon itself was at the very end of the cliffs, tucked in against the sea. It looked almost too quaint from here, like a model in a black and white Hollywood film.

He came to a break in the path, a second, much rougher track leading away from the sea and across the fields. His instincts would have told him to go straight ahead, but a footpath sign pointed to the right. There was something strange about the sign. Alex hesitated for a moment, wondering what it was. Then he dismissed it. He was walking in the countryside and the sun was shining. What could possibly be wrong? He followed the sign.

The path continued for about another quarter of a mile, then dipped down into a hollow. Here the grass was almost as tall as Alex, rising up all around him, a shimmering green cage. A bird suddenly erupted in front of him, a ball of brown feathers that spun round on itself before taking flight. Something had disturbed it. And that was when Alex heard the sound – an engine getting closer. A tractor? No. It was too high-pitched and moving too fast.

Alex knew he was in danger the same way an animal does. There was no need to ask why or how. Danger was simply there. And even as the dark shape appeared, crashing through the grass, he was throwing himself to one side, knowing – too late now – what it was that had been wrong about the second footpath sign. It had been brand-new. The first sign, the one that had led him off the road, had been weather-beaten and old. Someone had deliberately led him away from the correct path and brought him here.

To the killing field.

He hit the ground and rolled into a ditch on one side. The vehicle burst through the grass, its front wheel almost touching his head. Alex caught a glimpse of a squat black thing with four fat tyres, a cross between a miniature tractor and a motorbike. It was being ridden by a hunched-up figure in grey leathers, with helmet and goggles. Then it was gone, thudding down into the grass on the other side of him and disappearing instantly, as if a curtain had been drawn.

Alex scrambled to his feet and began to run. There were two of them. He knew what they were now. He'd ridden similar things himself, on holiday, in the sand-dunes of Death Valley, Nevada. Kawasaki four by fours, powered by 400cc engines with automatic transmission. Quad bikes.

They were circling him like wasps. A drone, then a scream, and the second bike was in front of him, roaring towards him, cutting a swathe through the grass. Alex hurled himself out of its path, once again crashing into the ground, almost dislocating his shoulder. Wind and engine fumes whipped across his face.

He had to find somewhere to hide. But he was in the middle of a field and there was nowhere –

apart from the grass itself. Desperately, he fought through it, the blades scratching at his face, half-blinding him as he tried to find his way back to the main path. He needed other people. Whoever had sent these machines (and now he remembered Mr Grin talking on his mobile phone), they couldn't kill him if there were witnesses around.

But there was no one, and they were coming for him again ... together this time. Alex could hear the engines, whining in unison, coming up fast behind him. Still running, he glanced over his shoulder and saw them, one on each side, seemingly about to overtake him. It was only the glint of the sun and the sight of the grass slicing itself in half that revealed the horrible truth. The two bikers had stretched a length of cheese-wire between them.

Alex threw himself head-first, landing flat on his stomach. The cheese-wire whipped over him. If he had still been standing up, it would have cut him in half.

The quad bikes separated, arcing away from each other. At least that meant they must have dropped the wire. Alex had twisted his knee in the last fall and he knew it was only a matter of time before they cornered him and finished him off. Half-limping, he ran forward, searching for somewhere to hide or something to defend himself with. Apart from some money, he had nothing in his pockets, not even a penknife. The engines were distant now, but he knew they would be closing in again at any moment. And what would it be next time? More cheese-wire? Or something worse?

It was worse. Much worse. There was the roar of an engine and then a billowing cloud of red fire exploded over the grass, blazing it to a crisp. Alex felt it singe his shoulders, yelled and threw himself to one side. One of the riders was carrying a flame-thrower! He had just aimed a bolt of fire eight metres long, meaning to burn Alex alive. And he had almost succeeded. Alex was saved only by the narrow ditch he'd landed in. He hadn't even seen it until he had thudded to the ground, into the damp soil, the jet of flame licking at the air just above him. It had been close. There was a horrible smell: his own hair. The fire had singed the ends.

Choking, his face streaked with dirt and sweat, he clambered out of the ditch and ran blindly forward. He had no idea where he was going any more. He only knew that in a few seconds the quad would be back. He had taken about ten paces before he realized he had reached the edge of the field. There was a warning sign and an electrified fence stretching as far as he could see. But for the buzzing sound the fence was making, he would have run right into it. The fence was almost invisible, and the quad bikers, moving fast towards him, would be unable to hear the warning sound over their own engines...

He stopped and turned round. About fifty metres away from him, the grass was being flattened by the still invisible quad as it made its next charge. But this time Alex waited. He stood there, balancing on the heels of his feet, like a matador. Twenty metres, ten... Now he was staring straight into the goggles of the rider, saw the man's uneven teeth as he smiled, still gripping the flame-thrower. The quad smashed down the last barrier of grass and leapt on to him ... except that Alex was no longer there. He had dived to one side and, too late, the driver saw the fence and rocketed on, straight into it. The man screamed as the wire caught him around the neck, almost garrotting him. The bike twisted in mid-air, then crashed down. The man fell into the grass and lay still.

He had torn the fence out of the ground. Alex ran over to the man and examined him. For a moment he thought it might be Yassen, but it was a younger man, dark-haired, ugly. Alex had never seen him before. The man was unconscious but still breathing. The flame-thrower lay, extinguished, on the ground beside him. Behind him, he heard the other bike, some distance away but closing. Whoever these people were, they had tried to run him down, cut him in half and incinerate him. He had to find a way out before they got really serious.

He ran over to the abandoned quad, which had come to rest lying on its side. He heaved it up again, jumped on to the seat and pressed the starter. The engine sprang into life. At least there were no gears to worry about. Alex twisted the accelerator and gripped the handlebars as the machine jolted him forward.

And now he was slicing through the grass, which became a green blur as the quad carried him back towards the footpath. He couldn't hear the other bike but hoped that the rider would have no idea what had happened and so wouldn't be following him. His bones rattled as the quad hit a rut and bounced upwards. He had to be careful. Lose his concentration for a second and he would be on his back.

He cut through another green curtain and savagely pulled on the handlebars to bring himself round. He had found the footpath – and also the edge of the cliff. Just three metres more and he would have launched himself into space and down to the rocks below. For a few seconds he sat where he was, the engine idling. That was when the other quad appeared. Somehow the second rider must have guessed what had happened. He had reached the footpath and was facing Alex, about two hundred metres away. Something glinted in his hand, resting on the handlebar. He was carrying a gun.

Alex looked back the way he had walked. It was no good. The path was too narrow. By the time he had turned the quad round, the armed man would have reached him. One shot and it would all be over. Could he go back into the grass? No, for the same reason. He had to move forward, even if that meant heading for a straight-on collision with the other quad.

Why not? Maybe there was no other way.

The man gunned his engine and spurted forward. Alex did the same. Now the two of them were racing towards each other down a narrow path, a bank of earth and rock suddenly rising up to form a barrier on one side and the edge of the cliff on the other. There wasn't enough room for them to pass. They could stop or they could crash

... but if they were going to stop they had to do it in the next ten seconds.

The quads were getting closer and closer, moving faster all the time. The man couldn't shoot him now, not without losing control. Far below, the waves glittered silver, breaking against the rocks. The edge of the cliff flashed by. The noise of the other quad filled Alex's ears. The wind rushed into him, hammering at his chest and face. It was like the old-fashioned game of chicken. One of them had to stop. One of them had to get out of the way.

Three, two, one...

It was the enemy who finally broke. He was less than five metres away, so close that Alex could make out the perspiration on his forehead. Just when it seemed that a crash was inevitable, he twisted his quad and swerved off the path, up on to the embankment. At the same time, he tried to fire his gun. But he was too late. His quad was slanting, tipping over on to just two of its wheels, and the shot went wild. The man yelled out. Firing the gun had caused him to lose what little control he had left. He fought with the quad, trying to bring it back on to four wheels. It hit a rock and bounced upwards, landed briefly on the footpath, then continued over the edge of the cliff.

Alex had felt the machine rush past him, but he had seen little more than a blur. He had shuddered to a halt and turned round just in time to watch the other quad fly into the air. The man, still screaming, had managed to separate himself from the bike on the way down, but the two of them hit the water at the same moment. The quad sank a few seconds before the man.

Who had sent him? It was Nadia Vole who had suggested the walk, but it was Mr Grin who had actually seen him leave. Mr Grin had given the order – he was sure of it.

Alex took the quad all the way to the end of the path. The sun was still shining as he walked down into the little fishing village, but he couldn't enjoy it. He was angry with himself because he knew he'd made too many mistakes.

He should have been dead now, he knew. Only luck and a low-voltage electric fence had managed to keep him alive.

DOZMARY MINE

Alex walked through Port Tallon, past the Fisherman's Arms pub and up the cobbled street towards the library. It was the middle of the afternoon but the village seemed to be asleep; the boats bobbing in the harbour, the streets and pavements empty. A few seagulls wheeled lazily over the rooftops, uttering the usual mournful cries. The air smelled of salt and dead fish.

The library was red-brick, Victorian, sitting self-importantly at the top of a hill. Alex pushed open the heavy swing-door and went into a room with a tiled, chessboard floor and about fifty shelves fanning out from a central reception area. Six or seven people were sitting at tables, working. A man in a thickly knitted jersey was reading *Fisherman's Week*. Alex went over to the reception desk. There was the inevitable sign – SILENCE PLEASE. Beneath it a smiling, round-faced woman sat reading *Crime and Punishment*.

"Can I help you?" Despite the sign, she had such a loud voice that everyone looked up when she spoke.

"Yes..."

Alex had come here because of a chance remark made by Herod Sayle. He had been talking about Ian Rider. *Spent half his time in the village. In the port, the post office, the library.* Alex had already seen the post office, another old-fashioned building near the port. He didn't think he'd learn anything there. But the library? Maybe Rider had come here looking for information. Maybe the librarian would remember him.

"I had a friend staying in the village," Alex said. "I was wondering if he came here. His name's Ian Rider."

"Rider with an I or a Y? I don't think we have any Riders at all." The woman tapped a few keys on her computer, then shook her head. "No."

"He was staying at Sayle Enterprises," Alex said. "He was about forty, thin, fair hair. He drove a BMW."

"Oh yes." The librarian smiled. "He did come

here a couple of times. A nice man. Very polite. I knew he didn't come from around here. He was looking for a book—"

"Do you remember which book?"

"Of course I do. I can't always remember faces, but I never forget a book. He was interested in viruses."

"Viruses?"

"Yes. That's what I said. He wanted some information..."

A computer virus! This might change everything. A computer virus was the perfect act of sabotage: invisible and instantaneous. A single blip written into the software and every single piece of information in the Stormbreaker software could be destroyed at any time. But Herod Sayle couldn't possibly want to damage his own creation. That would make no sense at all. So maybe Alex had been wrong about him from the very start. Maybe Sayle had no idea what was really going on.

"I'm afraid I couldn't help him," the librarian continued. "This is only a small library and our grant's been cut for the third year running." She sighed. "Anyway, he said he'd get some books sent down from London. He told me he had a box at the post office..."

That made sense too. Ian Rider wouldn't have wanted information sent to Sayle Enterprises, where it could be intercepted.

"Was that the last time you saw him?" Alex asked.

"No. He came back about a week later. He must have got what he wanted because this time he wasn't looking for books about viruses. He was interested in local affairs."

"What sort of local affairs?"

"Cornish local history. Shelf CL." She pointed. "He spent an afternoon looking in one of the books and then he left. He hasn't been back since then, which is a shame. I was rather hoping he'd join the library. It would be nice to have a new member."

Local history. That wasn't going to help him. Alex thanked the librarian and made for the door. His hand was just reaching out for the handle when he remembered.

CL 475/19.

He reached into his pocket and took out the square of paper he had found in his bedroom. Sure enough, the letters were the same. CL. They weren't showing a grid reference. CL was the label on a book!

Alex went over to the shelf the librarian had

shown him. Books grow old faster when they're not being read and the ones gathered here were long past retirement, leaning tiredly against one another for support. CL 475/19 – the number was printed on the spine – was called *Dozmary: The Story of Cornwall's Oldest Mine.*

He carried it over to a table, opened it and quickly skimmed through it, wondering why a history of Cornish tin should have been of interest to Ian Rider. The story it told was a familiar one.

The mine had been owned by the Dozmary family for eleven generations. In the nineteenth century there had been four hundred mines in Cornwall. By the early nineteen nineties there were only three. Dozmary was still one of them. The price of tin had collapsed and the mine itself was almost exhausted, but there was no other work in the area and the family had continued running it even though the mine was quickly exhausting them. In 1991, Sir Rupert Dozmary, the last owner, had quietly slipped away and blown his brains out. He was buried in the local churchyard in a coffin made, it was said, of tin.

His children had closed down the mine, selling the land above it to Sayle Enterprises. The mine itself was sealed off, with several of the tunnels now underwater.

The book contained a number of old black and white photographs: pit ponies and old-fashioned lanterns. Groups of figures standing with axes and lunch boxes. Now all of them would be under the ground themselves. Flicking through the pages, Alex came to a map showing the layout of the tunnels at the time when the mine was closed.

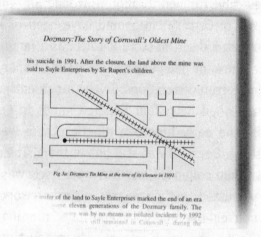

Dozmary: The Story of Cornwall's Oldest Mine

his suicide in 1991. After the closure, the land above the mine was sold to Sayle Enterprises by Sir Rupert's children.

Fig 3a: Dozmary Tin Mine at the time of its closure in 1991

...sfer of the land to Sayle Enterprises marked the end of an era ...me eleven generations of the Dozmary family. The ...ry was by no means an isolated incident: by 1992 ...still remained in Cornwall , during the

It was hard to be sure of the scale, but there was a labyrinth of shafts, tunnels and railway lines running for miles underground. Go down into the utter blackness of the underground and you'd be lost instantly. Had Ian Rider made his way into Dozmary? If so, what had he found?

Alex remembered the corridor at the foot of the metal staircase. The dark brown, unfinished walls and the light bulbs hanging on their wires had reminded him of something, and suddenly he knew what it was. The corridor must be nothing more than one of the tunnels from the old mine! Suppose Ian Rider had also gone down the staircase. Like Alex, he had been confronted with the locked metal door and had been determined to find his way past it. But he had recognized the corridor for what it was – and that was why he had come back to the library. He had found a book on the Dozmary Mine – this book. The map had shown him a way to the other side of the door.

And he had made a note of it!

Alex took out the diagram that Ian Rider had drawn and laid it on the page, on top of the printed map. Holding the two sheets together, he held them up to the light.

This was what he saw.

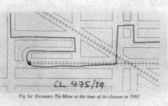

CL 475/19

Fig 5a: Dozmary Tin Mine at the time of its closure in 1991

The lines that Rider had drawn on the sheet fitted exactly over the shafts and tunnels of the mine, showing the way through. Alex was certain of it. If he could find the entrance to Dozmary, he could follow the map through to the other side of the metal door.

Ten minutes later he left the library with a photocopy of the page. He went down to the harbour and found one of those maritime stores that seem to sell anything and everything. Here he bought himself a powerful torch, a jersey, a length of rope and a box of chalk.

Then he climbed back into the hills.

Back on the quad, Alex raced across the cliff tops with the sun already sinking in the west. Ahead of him he could see the single chimney and crumbling tower that he hoped would mark the entrance to the Kerneweck Shaft, which took its name from the ancient language of Cornwall. According to the map, this was where he should begin. At least the quad had made his life easier. It would have taken him an hour to reach it on foot.

He was running out of time and he knew it. Already the Stormbreakers would have begun leaving the plant, and in less than twenty-four hours the Prime Minister would be activating them. If the software really had been infected with some sort of virus, what would happen?

Some sort of humiliation for both Sayle and the British Government? Or worse?

And how did a computer bug tie in with what he had seen the night before? Whatever the submarine had been delivering at the jetty, it couldn't be anything to do with computers. The silver boxes with their vacuum seals looked like something out of Star Wars. And you don't shoot a man for dropping a hard drive.

Alex parked the quad next to the tower and went in through an arched doorway. At first he thought he must have made some sort of mistake. The building looked more like a ruined church than the entrance to a mine. Other people had been here before him. There were a few crumpled beer cans and old crisp packets on the floor and the usual graffiti on the walls. JRH WAS HERE. NICK LOVES CASS. Visitors leaving the worst parts of themselves behind in fluorescent paint.

His foot came down on something that clanged and he saw that he was standing on a metal trapdoor, set into the concrete floor. Grass and weeds were sprouting round the edges, but putting his hand against the crack he could feel a draught of air rising from below. This must be the entrance to the shaft.

The trapdoor was bolted down with a heavy

padlock, several centimetres thick. Alex swore under his breath. He had left the zit cream back in his room. The cream would have eaten through the bolt in seconds, but he didn't have the time to go all the way back to Sayle Enterprises to get it. He knelt down and shook the padlock in frustration. To his surprise, it swung open in his hand. Somebody had been here before him. Ian Rider – it had to be. He must have managed to unlock it, and hadn't fully closed it again so that it would be ready when he came back.

Alex pulled the padlock out and grabbed hold of the trapdoor. It took all his strength to pull it up and as he did so, a blast of cold air hit him in the face. The trapdoor clanged back and he found himself looking into a black hole that stretched further than the daylight could reach. Alex shone his torch into the hole. The beam went about fifty metres, but the shaft went further. He found a pebble and dropped it in. At least ten seconds passed before the pebble rattled against something far below.

A rusty ladder ran down the side of the shaft. Alex checked that the quad was out of sight, then looped the rope over his shoulder and shoved the torch into his belt. He didn't enjoy climbing into the hole. The metal rungs were ice-cold against his hands, and his shoulders had barely sunk beneath the level of the ground before the light was blotted out and he felt himself being sucked into a darkness so total that he couldn't even be sure he had eyes. But he couldn't climb *and* hold on to the torch. He just had to feel his way, a hand then a foot, descending further and ever further until at last his heel struck the ground and he knew he had reached the bottom of the Kerneweck Shaft.

He looked up. He could just make out the entrance he had climbed through – small, round, as distant as the moon. Breathing heavily, trying to fight off the sense of claustrophobia, he pulled out the torch and flicked it on. The beam leapt out of his hand, pointing the way ahead and throwing pure, white light on to his immediate surroundings. Alex was at the start of a long tunnel, the uneven walls and ceiling held back by wooden beams. The floor was already damp and a sheen of salt water hung in the air. It was cold in the mine. He had known it would be and before he moved he pulled on the jersey he had bought, then chalked a large X on the wall. That had been a good idea too. Whatever happened down here, he wanted to be sure he could find the way back.

At last he was ready. He took two steps forward,

away from the vertical shaft and into the start of the tunnel, and immediately felt the weight of the solid rock, soil and remaining streaks of tin bearing down on him. It was horrible here. It really was like being buried alive, and it took all his strength to force himself on. After about fifty paces he came to a second tunnel, branching off to the left. He took out the photocopied map and examined it in the torchlight. According to Ian Rider, this was where he had to turn off. He swung the torch round and followed the tunnel, which slanted downwards, taking him deeper and deeper into the earth.

There was absolutely no sound in the mine apart from his own rasping breath, the crunch of his footsteps and the quickening thud of his heart. It was as if the blackness was wiping out sound as well as vision. Alex opened his mouth and called out, just to hear something. But his voice sounded small and only reminded him of the huge weight above his head. This tunnel was in bad repair. Some of the beams had snapped and fallen in and as he passed, a trickle of gravel hit his neck and shoulders, reminding him that the Dozmary mine had been kept locked for a reason. It was a hellish place. It could collapse at any time.

The path took him ever deeper. He could feel the pressure pounding in his ears and the darkness seemed even thicker and more oppressive. He came to a tangle of iron and wire, some sort of machine long ago buried and forgotten. He climbed over it too quickly, cutting his leg on a piece of jagged metal. He stood still for a few seconds, forcing himself to slow down. He knew he couldn't panic. *If you panic, you'll get lost. Think what you're doing. Be careful. One step at a time.*

"OK. OK..." He whispered the words to reassure himself, then continued forward.

Now he emerged into a sort of wide, circular chamber, formed by the meeting of six different tunnels, all coming together in a star shape. The widest of these slanted in from the left with the remains of a railway track. He swung the torch and picked out a couple of wooden wagons which must have been used to carry equipment down or tin back up to the surface. Checking the maps, he was tempted to follow the railway, which seemed to offer a short cut across the route that Ian Rider had drawn. But he decided against it. His uncle had turned the corner and gone back on himself. There had to be a reason. Alex made another two chalk crosses, one for the tunnel he had left, another for the one he was entering. He went on.

This new tunnel quickly became lower and narrower until Alex couldn't walk unless he crouched. The floor was very wet here, with pools of water reaching his ankles. He remembered how near he was to the sea and that brought another unpleasant thought. What time was high tide? And when the water rose, what would happen inside the mine? Alex suddenly had a vision of himself trapped in blackness with the water rising up his chest, his neck, over his face. He stopped and forced himself to think of something else. Down here, on his own, far beneath the surface of the earth, he couldn't make an enemy of his imagination.

The tunnel curved, then joined a second railway line, this one bent and broken, covered here and there in rubble which must have fallen from above. But the metal tracks made it easier to move forward, picking up and reflecting the torch. Alex followed them all the way to a junction with the main railway. It had taken him thirty minutes and he was almost back where he had started but, shining the torch around him, he saw why Ian Rider had sent him the long way round. There had been a tunnel collapse. About thirty metres up the line, the main railway was blocked.

He crossed the tracks, still following the maps, and stopped. He looked at the paper, then again at the way ahead. It was impossible. And yet there was no mistake.

He had come to a small, round tunnel dipping steeply down. But after ten metres the tunnel simply stopped, with what looked like a sheet of metal barring the way. Alex picked up a stone and threw it. There was a splash. Now he understood. The tunnel was completely submerged in water as black as ink. The water had risen up to the ceiling of the tunnel so that, even assuming he could swim in temperatures that must be close to zero, he would be unable to breathe. After all his hard work, after all the time he had spent underground, there was no way forward.

Alex turned. He was about to leave, but even as he swung the torch round, the beam picked up something lying in a heap on the ground. He went over to it and leaned down. It was a diver's dry suit and it looked brand-new. Alex walked back to the water's edge and examined it with the torch. This time he saw something else. A rope had been tied to a rock. It slanted diagonally into the water and disappeared. Alex knew what it meant.

Ian Rider had swum through the submerged

tunnel. He had worn a dry suit and he had managed to fix a rope to guide him through. Obviously he had planned to come back. That was why he had left the padlock open. It seemed that once again Alex had been helped by the dead man. The question was, did he have the nerve to go on?

He picked up the dry suit. It was too big for him, although it would probably keep out the worst of the chill. But the cold wasn't the only problem. The tunnel might run for ten metres. It might run for a hundred. How could he be sure that Ian Rider hadn't used scuba equipment to swim through? If Alex went down there, into the water, and ran out of breath halfway, he would drown. Pinned underneath the rock in the freezing blackness. He couldn't imagine a worse way to die.

But he had come so far, and according to the map he was nearly there. Alex swore. This was not fun. At that moment he wished he had never heard of Alan Blunt, Sayle Enterprises or the Stormbreaker. But he couldn't go back. If his uncle had done it, so could he. Gritting his teeth, he pulled on the dry suit. It was cold, clammy and uncomfortable. He zipped it up. He hadn't taken off his ordinary clothes and perhaps that helped. The suit was loose in places, but he was sure it would keep the water out.

Moving quickly now, afraid that if he hesitated he would change his mind, Alex approached the water's edge. He reached out and took the rope in one hand. It would be faster swimming with both hands, but he didn't dare risk it. Getting lost in the underwater tunnel would be as bad as running out of air. The result would be exactly the same. He had to keep hold of the rope to allow it to guide him through. Alex took several deep breaths, hyperventilating and oxygenating his blood, knowing it would give him a few precious extra seconds. Then he plunged in.

The cold was ferocious, a hammer blow that nearly forced the air out of his lungs. The water pounded at his head, swirling round his nose and eyes. His fingers were instantly numb. His whole system felt the shock, but the dry suit was holding, sealing in at least some of his body warmth. Clinging to the rope, he kicked forward. He had committed himself. There could be no going back.

Pull, kick. Pull, kick. Alex had been underwater for less than a minute but already his lungs were feeling the strain. The roof of the tunnel was scraping his shoulders and he was afraid that it would tear through the dry suit and gouge his skin as well. But he didn't dare slow down. The freezing cold was sucking the strength out of him. Pull and kick. Pull and kick. How long had he been under? Ninety seconds? A hundred? His eyes were tight shut, but if he opened them there would be no difference. He was in a black, swirling, freezing version of hell. And his breath was running out.

He pulled himself forward along the rope, burning the skin off the palms of his hands. He must have been swimming for almost two minutes. It felt closer to ten. He *had* to open his mouth and breathe, even if it was water that would rush into his throat... A silent scream exploded inside him. Pull, kick. Pull, kick. And then the rope tilted upwards and he felt his shoulders come clear, and his mouth was wrenched open in a great gasp as he breathed air and knew that he had made it, perhaps with only seconds to spare.

But made it to where?

Alex couldn't see anything. He was floating in utter darkness, unable to see even where the water ended. He had left the torch at the other side, but he knew that even if he wanted to he didn't have the strength to go back. He had followed the trail left by a dead man. It was only now that he realized it might lead only to the grave.

BEHIND THE DOOR

Alex swam slowly forward, completely blind, afraid that at any moment he would crack his skull against rock. Despite the dry suit, he was beginning to feel the chill of the water and knew that he had to find his way out soon. His hand brushed against something but his fingers were too numb to tell what it was. He reached out and pulled himself forward. His feet touched the bottom. And it was then that he realized. He could see. Somehow, from somewhere, light was seeping into the area beyond the submerged tunnel.

Slowly, his vision adjusted itself. Waving his hand in front of his face, he could just make out his fingers. He was holding on to a wooden beam, a collapsed roof support. He closed his eyes, then opened them again. The darkness had retreated, showing him a crossroads cut into the rock, the meeting place of three tunnels. The fourth, behind him, was the one that was flooded. As vague as the light was, it gave him strength. Using the beam as a makeshift jetty, he clambered on to the rock. At the same time, he became aware of a soft throbbing sound. He couldn't be sure if it was near or far, but he remembered what he had heard under Block D, in front of the metal door, and he knew that he had arrived.

He stripped off the dry suit. Fortunately, it had kept the water out. The main part of his body was dry, but ice-cold water was still dripping out of his hair, down his neck, and his trainers and socks were sodden. When he moved forward his feet squelched and he had to take his trainers off and shake them out before he could go on. Ian Rider's map was still folded in his pocket, but he no longer had any need of it. All he had to do was follow the light.

He went straight forward to another intersection, then turned right. The light was so bright now that he could actually make out the colour of the rock – dark brown and grey. The throbbing was also getting louder and Alex could feel a rush of warm air streaming down towards him. He moved forward cautiously, wondering what he was about to come to. He turned a corner and suddenly the rock on both sides gave way to new brick, with metal grilles set at intervals just above the level of the floor. The old mine shaft had been converted. It was being used as the outlet for some sort of air-conditioning system. The light that had guided Alex was coming out of the grilles.

He knelt beside the first of these and looked through into a large, white-tiled room, a laboratory with complicated glass and steel equipment laid out over work surfaces. The room was empty. Tentatively, Alex took hold of the grille, but it was firmly secured, bolted into the rock face. The second grille belonged to the same room. It was also screwed on tight. Alex continued up the tunnel to a third grille. This one looked into a storage room filled with the silver boxes that Alex had seen being delivered by the submarine the night before.

He took the grille in both hands and pulled. It came away from the rock easily, and looking closer he understood why. Ian Rider had been here ahead of him. He had cut through the bolts which had held it in place. Alex set the grille down silently. He felt sad. Ian Rider had found his way through the mine, drawn the map, swum through the submerged tunnel and opened the grille all on his own. Alex wouldn't have got nearly as far as this without his help, and he wished now that he had known his uncle a little better and perhaps admired him a little more before he died.

Carefully, he began to squeeze through the rectangular hole and lower himself into the room. At the last minute – lying on his stomach with his feet dangling below – he reached for the grille and set it back in place. Provided nobody looked too closely, they wouldn't see anything wrong. He dropped down to the ground and landed, catlike, on the balls of his feet. The throbbing was louder now, coming from somewhere outside. It would cover any noise he made. He went over to the nearest of the silver boxes and examined it. This time it clicked open in his hands, but when he looked inside it was empty. Whatever had been delivered was already in use.

He checked for cameras, then crossed to the door. It was unlocked. He opened it, one centimetre at a time, and peered out. The door led on to a wide corridor with an automatic sliding door at each end and a silver handrail running its full length.

"1900 hours. Red shift to assembly line. Blue shift to decontamination."

The voice rang out over a loudspeaker system, neither male nor female; emotionless, inhuman. Alex glanced at his watch. It was already seven o'clock in the evening. It had taken him longer than he'd thought to get through the mine. He stole forward. It wasn't exactly a passage that he had found. It was more an observation platform. He reached the rail and looked down.

Alex hadn't had any idea what he would find behind the metal door, but what he was seeing now was far beyond anything he could have imagined. It was a huge chamber, the walls – half naked rock, half polished steel – lined with computer equipment, electronic meters, machines that blinked and flickered with a life of their own. It was staffed by forty or fifty people, some in white coats, others in overalls, all wearing armbands of different colours: red, yellow, blue and green. Arc lights beamed down from above. Armed guards stood at each doorway, watching the work with blank faces.

For this was where the Stormbreakers were being assembled. The computers were being slowly carried in a long, continuous line along a conveyor-belt, past the various scientists and technicians. The strange thing was that they already looked finished ... and of course they had to be. Sayle had told him. They were actually being shipped out during the course of that afternoon and night. So what last-minute adjustment was being made here in this secret factory? And why was so much of the production line hidden away? What Alex had seen on his tour of Sayle Enterprises had only been the tip of the iceberg. The main body of the factory was here, underground.

He looked more closely. He remembered the Stormbreaker that he had used, and now he noticed something that he hadn't seen then. A strip of plastic had been drawn back in the casing above each of the screens to reveal a small compartment, cylindrical and about five centimetres deep. The computers were passing underneath a bizarre machine – cantilevers, wires and hydraulic arms. Opaque silver test-tubes were being fed along a narrow cage, moving forward as if to greet the computers: one tube for each computer. There was a meeting point. With infinite precision, the tubes were lifted out, brought round and then dropped into the exposed compartments. After that, the Stormbreakers were accelerated forward. A second machine closed and heat-sealed the plastic strips. By the time the computers reached the end of the line, where they were packed into red and white Sayle Enterprises boxes, the compartments were completely invisible.

A movement caught his eye and Alex looked beyond the assembly line and through a huge window into the chamber next door. Two men in biohazard suits were walking clumsily together, as if in slow motion. They stopped. An alarm began to sound and suddenly they disappeared in a cloud of white steam. Alex remembered what he had just heard. Were they being decontaminated? But if the Stormbreaker was based on the round processor there couldn't possibly be any need for such an extreme – and anyway, this was like nothing Alex had ever seen before. If the men were being decontaminated, what were they being decontaminated from?

"Agent Gregorovich report to the Biocontainment Zone. This is a call for Agent Gregorovich."

A lean, fair-haired figure dressed in black detached himself from the assembly line and walked languidly towards a door that slid open to receive him. For the second time Alex found himself looking at the Russian contract killer,

Yassen Gregorovich. What was going on? Alex thought back to the submarine and the vacuum-sealed boxes. Of course. Yassen had brought the test-tubes that were even now being inserted into the computers. The test-tubes were some sort of weapon that he was using to sabotage them. No. That wasn't possible. Back in Port Tallon, the librarian had told him that Ian Rider had been asking for books about computer viruses...

Viruses.

Decontamination.

The Biocontainment Zone...

Understanding came – and with it, something cold and solid jabbing into the back of his neck. Alex hadn't even heard the door open behind him, but he slowly stiffened as a voice spoke softly into his ear.

"Stand up. Keep your hands by your sides. If you make any sudden moves, I'll shoot you in the head."

He looked slowly round. A single guard stood behind him, a gun in his hand. It was the sort of thing Alex had seen a thousand times in films and on television, and he was shocked by how different the reality was. The gun was a Browning automatic pistol and one twitch of the guard's finger would send a 9mm bullet shattering through his skull and into his brain. The very touch of it made him feel sick.

He stood up. The guard was in his twenties, pale-faced and puzzled. Alex had never seen him before – but more importantly, he had never seen Alex. He hadn't expected to come across a boy. That might help.

"Who are you?" he asked. "What are you doing here?"

"I'm staying with Mr Sayle," Alex said. He stared at the gun. "Why are you pointing that at me? I'm not doing anything wrong."

He sounded pathetic. Little boy lost. But it had the desired effect. The guard hesitated, slightly lowering the gun. At that moment Alex struck. It was another classic karate blow, this time twisting his body round and driving his elbow into the side of the guard's head, just below his ear. He had almost certainly knocked him out with the single punch, but he couldn't take chances and followed it through with a knee to the groin. The guard folded up, his pistol falling to the ground. Quickly, Alex dragged him back, away from the railing. He looked down. Nobody had seen what had happened.

But the guard wouldn't be unconscious long and Alex knew he had to get out of there – not just back up to ground level but out of Sayle Enterprises itself. He had to contact Mrs Jones. He still didn't know how or why, but he knew now that the Stormbreakers had been turned into killing machines. There were less than seventeen hours until the launch at the Science Museum. Somehow Alex had to stop it from happening.

He ran. The door at the end of the passage slid open and he found himself in a curving white corridor with windowless offices built into what must be yet more shafts of the Dozmary Mine. He knew he couldn't go back the way he had come. He was too tired and even if he could find his way through the mine, he'd never be able to manage the swim a second time. His only chance was the door that had first led him here. It led to the metal staircase that would bring him to D Block. There was a telephone in his room. Failing that, he could use the Nintendo DS to transmit a message. But MI6 had to know what he had found out.

He reached the end of the corridor, then ducked back as three guards appeared, walking together towards a set of double doors. Fortunately they hadn't seen him. Nobody knew he was there. He was going to be all right.

And then the alarm went off. A klaxon barking electronically along the corridors, leaping out from the corners, echoing everywhere. Overhead, a light began to flash red. The guards wheeled round and saw Alex. Unlike the guard on the observation platform, they didn't hesitate. As Alex dived head-first through the nearest door, they brought up their machine-guns and fired. Bullets slammed into the wall beside him and ricocheted along the passageway. Alex landed flat on his stomach and kicked out, slamming the door behind him. He straightened up, found a bolt and rammed it home. A second later there was an explosive hammering on the other side as the guards fired at the door. But it was solid metal. It would hold.

He was standing on a gantry leading down to a tangle of pipes and cylinders, like the boiler room of a ship. The alarm was as loud here as it had been by the main chamber. It seemed to be coming from everywhere. Alex leapt down the staircase three steps at a time and skidded to a halt, searching for a way out. He had a choice of three corridors, but then he heard the rattle of feet and knew that his choice had just become two. He wished now that he had thought to pick up the Browning automatic. He was alone and unarmed. The only duck in the shooting gallery, with guns everywhere and no way out. Was this what MI6 had trained him for? If so, eleven days hadn't been enough.

He ran on, weaving in and out of the pipes, trying every door he came to. A room with more biohazard suits hanging on hooks. A shower room. Another, larger laboratory with a second door leading out and, in the middle, a glass tank shaped like a barrel and filled with green liquid. Tangles of rubber tubing sprouting out of the tank. Trays filled with test-tubes all around.

The barrel-shaped tank. The trays. Alex had seen them before – as vague outlines on his Nintendo. He must have been standing on the other side of the second door. He ran over to it. It was locked from the inside, electronically, by the glass identification plate against the wall. He would never be able to open it. He was trapped.

Footsteps approached. Alex just had time to hide himself on the floor, underneath one of the work surfaces, before the first door was thrown open and two more guards ran into the laboratory. They took a quick look around – without seeing him.

"Not here!" one of them said.

"You'd better go up!"

One guard walked out the way he had come. The other went over to the second door and placed his hand on the glass panel. There was a green glow and the door buzzed loudly. The guard threw it open and disappeared. Alex rolled forward as the door swung shut and just managed to get his hand into the crack. He waited a moment, then stood up. He pulled the door open. As he had hoped, he was looking out into the unfinished passageway where he had been surprised by Nadia Vole.

The guard had already gone on ahead. Alex slipped out, closing the door behind him, cutting off the sound of the klaxon. He made his way up the metal stairs and through a swing-door. He was grateful to find himself back in the fresh air. The sun had already set, but across the lawn the airstrip was ablaze, artificially illuminated by the sort of lights Alex had seen on football pitches. There were about a dozen lorries parked next to each other. Men were loading them up with heavy, square, red and white boxes. The cargo plane that Alex had seen when he arrived rumbled down the runway and lurched into the air.

Alex knew that he was looking at the end of the assembly line. The red and white boxes were the same ones he had seen in the underground chamber. The Stormbreakers, complete with their deadly secret, were being loaded up and delivered. By morning they would be all over the country.

Keeping low, he ran past the fountain and across the grass. He thought about making for the main gate, but he knew that was hopeless. The guards would have been alerted. They'd be waiting for him. Nor could he climb the perimeter fence, not with the razor wire stretched out across the top. No. His own room seemed the best answer. The telephone was there. And so were his only weapons: the few gadgets that Smithers had given him four days – or was it four years? – ago.

He entered the house through the kitchen, the same way he had left it the night before. It was only eight o'clock, but the whole place seemed to be deserted. He ran up the staircase and along the corridor to his room on the first floor. Slowly, he opened the door. It seemed his luck was holding out. There was nobody there. Without turning on the light, he went inside and snatched up the telephone. The line was dead. Never mind. He found his Nintendo, all four cartridges, his yo-yo and the zit cream and crammed them into his pockets. He had already decided not to stay there. It was too dangerous. He would find somewhere to hide out. Then he would use the Nemesis cartridge to contact MI6.

He went back to the door and opened it. With a shock he saw Mr Grin standing in the hallway, looking hideous with his white face, his ginger hair and his mauve, twisted smile. Alex reacted quickly, striking out with the heel of his right hand. But Mr Grin was quicker. He seemed to shimmy to one side, then his hand shot out, the side of it driving into Alex's throat. Alex gasped for breath but no breath came. The butler made an inarticulate sound and lashed out a second time. Alex got the impression that behind the livid scars he really was grinning, enjoying himself. He tried to avoid the blow, but Mr Grin's fist hit him square on the jaw. He was spun into the bedroom, falling backwards.

He never even remembered hitting the floor.

THE SCHOOL BULLY

They came for Alex the following morning.

He had spent the night handcuffed to a radiator in a small, dark room with a single barred window. It might once have been a coal cellar. When Alex opened his eyes, the grey, first light of the morning was just creeping in. He closed them and opened them again. His head was thumping and the side of his face was swollen where Mr Grin had hit him. His arms were twisted behind him and the tendons in his shoulders were on fire. But worse than all this was his sense of failure. It was 1st April, the day when the Stormbreakers would be unleashed. And Alex was helpless. He was the April fool.

It was just before nine o'clock when the door opened and two guards came in with Mr Grin behind them. The handcuffs were unlocked and Alex was forced to his feet. Then, with a guard holding him on each side, he was marched out of the room and up a flight of stairs. He was still in Sayle's house. The stairs led to the hall with its huge painting of Judgement Day. Alex looked at the figures, writhing in agony on the canvas. If he was right, the image would soon be repeated all over Britain. And it would happen in just three hours' time.

The guards half-dragged him through a doorway and into the room with the aquarium. There was a high-backed wooden chair in front of it. Alex was forced to sit down. His hands were cuffed behind him again. The guards left. Mr Grin remained.

He heard the sound of feet on the spiral staircase, saw the leather shoes coming down before he saw the man who wore them. Then Herod Sayle appeared, dressed in an immaculate pale grey silk suit. Blunt and the people at MI6 had been suspicious of the Middle-Eastern multi-millionaire from the very start. They'd always thought he had something to hide. But even they had never guessed the truth. He wasn't a friend of Alex's country. He was its worst enemy.

"Three questions," Sayle snapped. His voice

was utterly cold. "Who are you? Who sent you here? How much do you know?"

"I don't know what you're talking about," Alex said.

Sayle sighed. If there had been anything comical about him when Alex had first seen him, it had completely evaporated. His face was bored and business-like. His eyes were ugly, full of menace. "We have very little time," he said. "Mr Grin...?"

Mr Grin went over to one of the display cases and took out a knife, razor sharp with a serrated edge. He held it up close to his face, his eyes gleaming.

"I've already told you that Mr Grin used to be an expert with knives," Sayle continued. "He still is. Tell me what I want to know, Alex, or he will cause you more pain than you could begin to imagine. And don't try to lie to me, please. Just remember what happens to liars. Particularly to their tongues."

Mr Grin took a step closer. The blade flashed, catching the light.

"My name is Alex Rider," Alex said.

"Rider's son?"

"His nephew."

"Who sent you here?"

"The same people who sent him." There was no point lying. It didn't matter any more. The stakes had become too high.

"MI6?" Sayle laughed without any sign of humour. "They send fourteen-year-old boys to do their dirty work? Not very English, I'd have said. Not cricket, what?" He had adopted an exaggerated English accent. Now he walked forward and sat down behind the desk. "And what of my third question, Alex? How much have you found out?"

Alex shrugged, trying to look casual to hide the fear he was really feeling. "I know enough," he said.

"Go on."

Alex took a breath. Behind him, the jellyfish drifted past like a poisonous cloud. He could see it out of the corner of his eye. He tugged at the handcuffs, wondering if it would be possible to break the chair. There was a sudden flash and the knife that Mr Grin had been holding was suddenly quivering in the back of the chair, a hair's breadth from his head. The edge of the blade had actually nicked the skin of his neck. He felt a trickle of blood slide down over his collar.

"You're keeping us waiting," Herod Sayle said.

"All right. When my uncle was here, he got interested in viruses. He asked about them at the local library. I thought he was talking about computer viruses. That was the natural assumption. But I was wrong. I saw what you were doing last night. I heard them talking on the speaker system. Decontamination and Biocontainment Zones. They were talking about biological warfare. You've got hold of some sort of real virus. It came here in test-tubes, packed into silver boxes, and you've put them into the Stormbreakers. I don't know what happens next. I suppose when the computers are turned on, people die. They're in schools, so it'll be schoolchildren. Which means you're not the saint everyone thinks you are, Mr Sayle. A mass-murderer. A *bliddy* psycho, I suppose you might say."

Herod Sayle clapped his hands softly together. "You've done very well, Alex," he said. "I congratulate you. And I feel you deserve a reward. So I'm going to tell you everything. In a way it's appropriate that MI6 should have sent me a real English schoolboy. Because, you see, there's nothing in the world I hate more. Oh yes..." His face twisted with anger and for a moment Alex could see the madness, alive in his eyes. "You *bliddy* snobs with your stuck-up schools and your stinking English superiority! But I'm going to show you. I'm going to show you all!"

He stood up and walked over to Alex. "I came to this country forty years ago," he said. "I had no money. My family had nothing. But for a freak accident, I would probably have lived and died in Beirut. Better for you if I had! So much better!

"I was sent here by an American family, to be educated. They had friends in north London and I stayed with them while I went to the local school. You cannot imagine how I was feeling then. To be in London, which I had always believed to be the heart of civilization. To see such wealth and to know that I was going to be part of it! I was going to be English! To a child born in a Lebanese gutter, it was an impossible dream.

"But I was soon to learn the reality..." Sayle leaned forward and yanked the knife out of the chair. He tossed it to Mr Grin, who caught it and spun it in his hand.

"From the moment I arrived at the school, I was mocked and bullied. Because of my size. Because of the colour of my skin. Because I couldn't speak English well. Because I wasn't one of them. They had names for me. Herod Smell. Goat-boy. The Dwarf. And they played tricks on me. Drawing-pins on my chair. Books stolen and defaced. My trousers ripped off me and hung out on the flagpole, underneath the Union Jack." Sayle shook his head slowly. "I had loved that flag when I first came here," he said. "But in only weeks I came to hate it."

"Lots of people are bullied at school—" Alex began – and stopped as Sayle back-handed him viciously across the face.

"I haven't finished," he said. He was breathing heavily and there was spittle on his lower lip. Alex could see him reliving the past. And once again he was allowing the past to destroy him.

"There were plenty of bullies in that school," he said. "But there was one who was worse than any of them. He was a small, smarmy shrimp of a boy, but his parents were rich and he had a way with the other children. He knew how to talk his way around them ... a politician even then. Oh yes. He could be charming when he wanted to be. When there were teachers around. But the moment their backs were turned, he was on to me. He used to organize the others. *Let's get the Goat-boy. Let's push his head in the toilet.* He had a thousand ideas to make my life miserable and he never stopped thinking up more. All the time he goaded me and taunted me and there was nothing I could do because he was popular and I was a foreigner. And do you know who that boy grew up to be?"

"I think you're going to tell me anyway," Alex said.

"I am going to tell you. Yes. He grew up to be the *bliddy* Prime Minister!"

Sayle took out a white silk handkerchief and wiped his face. His bald head was gleaming with sweat. "All my life I've been treated the same way," he continued. "No matter how successful I've become, how much money I've made, how many people I've employed. I'm still a joke. I'm still Herod Smell, the Goat-boy, the Lebanese tramp. Well, for forty years I've been planning my revenge. And now, at last, my time has come. Mr Grin..."

Mr Grin went over to the wall and pressed a button. Alex half-expected the snooker table to rise out of the floor, but instead a panel slid up on every wall to reveal floor-to-ceiling television screens which immediately flickered into life. On one screen Alex could see the underground laboratory, on another the assembly line, on a third the airstrip with the last of the lorries on its way out. There were CCTV cameras everywhere and Sayle could see every corner of his kingdom without even leaving the room. No wonder Alex had been discovered so easily.

"The Stormbreakers are armed and ready. And yes, you're right, Alex. Each one contains what you might call a computer virus. But that, if you like, is my little April Fools' joke. Because the virus I'm talking about is a form of smallpox. Of course, Alex, it's been genetically modified to make it faster and stronger ... more lethal. A spoonful of the stuff would destroy a city. And my Stormbreakers hold much, much more than that.

"At the moment it's isolated, quite safe. But this afternoon there's going to be a bit of a party at the Science Museum. Every school in Britain will be joining in, with the schoolchildren gathered round their nice, shiny new computers. And at midday, on the stroke of twelve, my old friend the Prime Minister will make one of his smug, self-serving speeches and then he'll press a button. He thinks he'll be activating the computers and in a way he's right. Pressing the button will release the virus and by midnight tonight there will be no more schoolchildren in Britain, and the Prime Minister will weep as he remembers the day he first bullied Herod Sayle!"

"You're mad!" Alex exclaimed. "By midnight tonight you'll be in jail."

Sayle dismissed the thought with a wave of the

hand. "I think not. By the time anyone realizes what has happened, I'll be gone. I'm not alone in this, Alex. I have powerful friends who have supported me —"

"Yassen Gregorovich."

"You *have* been busy!" He seemed surprised that Alex knew the name. "Yassen is working for the people who have been helping me. Let's not mention any names or even nationalities. You'd be surprised how many countries there are in the world who loathe the English. Most of Europe, just to begin with. But anyway..." He clapped his hands and went back to his desk. "Now you know the truth. I'm glad I was able to tell you, Alex. You have no idea how much I loathe you. Even when you were playing that stupid game with me, the snooker, I was thinking how much pleasure it would give me to kill you. You're just like the boys I was at school with. Nothing has changed."

"You haven't changed," Alex said. His cheek was still smarting where Sayle had hit him. But he'd heard enough. "I'm sorry you were bullied at school," he said. "But lots of kids get bullied and they don't turn into nutcases. You're really sad, Mr Sayle. And your plan won't work. I've told MI6 everything I know. They'll be waiting for you at the Science Museum. So will the men in white coats."

Sayle giggled. "Forgive me if I don't believe you," he said. His face was suddenly stone. "And perhaps you forget that I warned you about lying to me."

Mr Grin took a step forward, flipping the knife over so that the blade landed in the flat of his hand.

"I'd like to watch you die," Sayle said. "Unfortunately, I have a pressing engagement in London." He turned to Mr Grin. "You can walk with me to the helicopter. Then come back here and kill the boy. Make it slow. Make it painful. We should have kept back some smallpox for him – but I'm sure you'll think of something much more creative."

He walked to the door, then stopped and turned to Alex.

"Goodbye, Alex. It wasn't a pleasure knowing you. But enjoy your death. And remember, you're only going to be the first…"

The door swung shut. Handcuffed to the chair with the jellyfish floating silently behind him, Alex was left alone.

DEEP WATER

Alex gave up trying to break free of the chair. His wrists were bruised and bloody where the chain had cut into him, and the cuffs were too tight. After thirty minutes, when Mr Grin still hadn't come back, he'd tried to reach the zit cream that Smithers had given him. He knew it would burn through the handcuffs in seconds and the worst thing was, he could actually feel it, where he had put it, in the zipped-up outer pocket of his combat trousers. But although his outstretched fingers were only a few centimetres away, try as he might, he couldn't reach it. It was enough to drive him mad.

He had heard the clatter of a helicopter taking off and knew that Herod Sayle must be on his way to London. Alex was still reeling from what he had heard. The multi-millionaire was completely insane. What he was planning was beyond belief, a mass-murder that would destroy Britain for generations to come. Alex tried to imagine what was about to happen. Tens of thousands of schoolchildren would be sitting in their classes, gathered round their new Stormbreakers, waiting for the moment – at midday exactly – when the Prime Minister would press his button and bring them on-line. But instead there would be a hiss and a small cloud of deadly smallpox vapour would be released into the crowded room. And minutes later, all over the country, the dying would begin. Alex had to close his mind to the thought. It was too horrible. And yet it was going to happen in just a couple of hours' time. He was the only person who could stop it. And here he was, tied down, unable to move.

The door opened. Alex twisted round, expecting to see Mr Grin, but it was Nadia Vole who hurried in, closing the door behind her. Her pale round face seemed flushed and her eyes, behind the glasses, were afraid. She came over to him.

"Alex!"

"What do you want?" Alex recoiled away from her as she leaned over him. Then there was a click and, to his astonishment, his hands came free.

She had unlocked the handcuffs! He stood up, wondering what was going on.

"Alex, listen to me," Vole said. The words were tumbling quickly and softly out of her yellow-painted lips. "We do not have much time. I am here to help you. I worked with your uncle – Herr Ian Rider." Alex stared at her in surprise. "Yes. I am on the same side as you."

"But nobody told me—"

"It was better for you not to know."

"But..." Alex was confused. "I saw you with the submarine. You knew what Sayle was doing..."

"There was nothing I could do. Not then. It's too hard to explain. We do not have time to argue. You want to stop him – no?"

"I need to find a phone."

"All the phones in the house are coded. You cannot use them. But I have a mobile in my office."

"Then let's go."

Alex was still suspicious. If Nadia Vole had known so much, why hadn't she tried to stop Sayle before? On the other hand, she had released him – and Mr Grin would be back any minute. He had no choice but to trust her. He followed her out of the room, round the corner and up a flight of stairs to a landing with a statue of a naked woman, some Greek goddess, in the corner. Vole paused for a moment, resting her hand against the statue's arm.

"What is it?" Alex asked.

"I feel dizzy. You go on. It's the first door on the left."

Alex went past her, along the landing. Out of the corner of his eye he saw her press down on the statue's arm. The arm moved ... a lever. By the time he knew he had been tricked, it was too late. He yelled out as the floor underneath him swung round on a hidden pivot. He tried to stop himself falling, but there was nothing he could do. He crashed on to his back and slid down, through the floor and into a black plastic tunnel which corkscrewed beneath him. As he went, he heard Nadia Vole laugh triumphantly – and then he was gone, desperately trying to find a purchase on the sides, wondering what would be at the end of his fall.

Five seconds later he found out. The corkscrew spat him out. He fell briefly through the air and splashed into cold water. For a moment he was blinded, fighting for air. Then he rose to the surface and found himself in a huge glass tank filled with water and rocks. That was when he realized, with horror, exactly where he was.

Vole had deposited him in the tank with the giant jellyfish: Herod Sayle's Portuguese man-o'-war. It was a miracle that he hadn't crashed right into it. He could see it in the far corner of the tank, its dreadful tentacles with their hundreds of stinging cells, twisting and spiralling in the water. There was nothing between him and it. Alex fought back the panic, forced himself to keep still. He realized that thrashing about in the water would only create the current that would bring the creature over to him. The jellyfish had no eyes. It didn't know he was there. It wouldn't ... couldn't attack.

But eventually it would reach him. The tank he was in was huge, at least ten metres deep and twenty or thirty metres long. The glass rose above the level of the water, far out of his reach. There was no way he could climb out. Looking down through the water, he could see light. He realized he was looking into the room he had just left, Herod Sayle's private office. There was a movement – everything was vague and distorted through the rippling water – and the door opened. Two figures walked in. Alex could barely make them out, but he knew who they were. Fräulein Vole and Mr Grin. They stood together in front of the tank. Vole was holding what looked like a mobile phone in her hand.

"I hope you can hear me, Alex." The German woman's voice rang out from a speaker somewhere above his head. "I am sure you will have seen by now that there is no way out of the tank. You can tread water. Maybe for one hour, maybe for two. Others have lasted for longer. What is the record, Mr Grin?"

"Ire naaargh!"

"Five and a half hours. Yes. But soon you will get tired, Alex. You will drown. Or perhaps it will be fast and you will drift into the embrace of our friend. You see him … no? It is not an embrace to be desired. It will kill you. The pain, I think, will be beyond the imagination of a child. It is a pity, Alex Rider, that MI6 chose to send you here. They will not be seeing you again."

The voice clicked off. Alex kicked in the water, keeping his head above the surface, his eyes fixed on the jellyfish. There was another blurred movement on the other side of the glass. Mr Grin had left the room. But Vole had stayed behind. She wanted to watch him die.

Alex looked up. The tank was lit from above by a series of neon strips, but they were too high to reach. Beneath him he heard a click and a soft, whirring sound. Almost at once he became aware that something had changed. The jellyfish was moving! He could see the translucent cone, with its dark mauve tip, heading towards him. Underneath the creature, the tentacles slowly danced.

He swallowed water and realized he had opened his mouth to cry out. Vole must have turned on the artificial current. That was what was making the jellyfish move. Desperately he kicked out with his feet, moving away from it, surging through the water on his back. One tentacle floated up and draped itself over his foot. If he hadn't been wearing trainers, he would have been stung. Could the stinging cells penetrate his clothes? Almost certainly. His trainers were the only protection he had.

He reached the back corner of the aquarium and paused there, one hand against the glass. He already knew that what Vole had said was true. If the jellyfish didn't get him, tiredness would. He had to fight every second to stay afloat, and sheer terror was sapping his strength.

The glass. He pushed against it, wondering if he could break it. Perhaps there was a way... He checked the distance between himself and the jellyfish, took a deep breath and dived down to the bottom of the pool. He could see Nadia Vole watching. Although she was a blur to him, he would be crystal clear to her. She didn't move, and Alex realized with despair that she had expected him to do just this.

He swam to the rocks and looked for one small enough to bring to the surface. But the rocks were too heavy. He found one about the size of his own head, but it refused to move. Vole hadn't tried to stop him because she knew that all the rocks were set in concrete. Alex was running out of breath. He twisted round and pushed himself up towards the surface, only seeing at the last second that the jellyfish had somehow drifted above him. He screamed, bubbles erupting out of his mouth. The tentacles were right over his head. Alex contorted his body and managed to stay down, flailing madly with his legs to propel himself sideways. His shoulder slammed into the nearest of the rocks and he felt the pain shudder through him. Clutching his arm in his hand, he backed into another corner and rose up, gasping for breath as his head broke through the surface of the water.

He couldn't break the glass. He couldn't climb out. He couldn't avoid the touch of the jellyfish for ever. Although he had brought all the gadgets Smithers had given him, none of them could help him.

And then Alex remembered the cream. He let go of his arm and ran a finger up the side of the aquarium. The tank was a marvel of engineering. Alex had no idea how much pressure the water was exerting on the huge plates of glass, but the whole thing was held together by a framework of iron girders that fitted round the corners on both the inside and outside of the glass, the metal faces held together by rivets.

Treading water, he unzipped his pocket and took out the tube. ZIT-CLEAN, FOR HEALTHIER SKIN. If Nadia Vole could see what he was doing, she would think he had gone mad. The jellyfish was drifting towards the back of the aquarium. Alex waited a few moments, then swam forward and dived for a second time.

There didn't seem to be very much of the cream given the thickness of the girders and the size of the tank, but Alex remembered the demonstration Smithers had given him, how little he had used. Would the cream even work underwater? There was no point worrying about that now. Alex held the tube against the metal corners at the front of the tank and did his best to squeeze a long line of cream all the way down the length of the metal, using his other hand to rub it in around the rivets.

He kicked his feet, propelling himself across to the other side. He didn't know how long he would have before the cream took effect, and anyway, Nadia Vole was already aware that something was wrong. Alex saw that she had stood up again and was speaking into a phone, perhaps calling for help.

He had used half the tube on one side of the tank. He used the second half on the other. The jellyfish was hovering above him, the tentacles reaching out as if to grab hold of him and stop him. How long had he been underwater? His heart was pounding. And what would happen when the metal broke?

He just had time to come up and take one breath before he found out.

Even underwater, the cream had burned through the rivets on the inside of the tank. The glass had separated from the girders and, with nothing to hold it back, the huge pressure of water had smashed it open like a door caught in the wind. Alex didn't see what happened. He didn't have time to think. The world spun and he was thrown forward as helpless as a cork in a waterfall. The next few seconds were a twisting nightmare of rushing water and exploding glass. Alex didn't dare open his eyes. He felt himself being hurled forward, slammed into something, then sucked back again. He was sure he had broken every bone in his body. Now he was underwater. He struggled to find air. His head broke through the surface but even so, when he finally opened his mouth, he was amazed he could actually breathe.

The front of the tank had blown off and thousands of litres of water had cascaded into Herod Sayle's office. The water had smashed the furniture and blown the windows out. It was still draining away through the floor. Bruised and dazed, Alex stood up, water curling round his ankles.

Where was the jellyfish?

He had been lucky that the two of them hadn't become tangled up in the sudden eruption of water. But it could still be close. There might still be enough water in Sayle's office to allow it to reach him. Alex backed into a corner of the room, his whole body taut. Then he saw it.

Nadia Vole had been less fortunate. She had been standing in front of the glass when the girders broke and she hadn't been able to get out of the way in time. She was lying on her back, her legs limp and broken. The Portuguese man-o'-war was all over her. Part of it was sitting on her face and she seemed to be staring at him through the quivering mass of jelly. Her yellow lips were drawn back in an endless scream. The tentacles were wrapped all around her, hundreds of stinging cells clinging to her arms and legs and chest. Feeling sick, Alex backed away to the door and staggered out into the corridor.

An alarm had gone off. He only heard it now, as sound and vision came back to him. The screaming of the siren shook him out of his dazed state. What time was it? Almost eleven o'clock. At least his watch was still working. But he was in Cornwall, at least a five-hour drive from London, and with the alarms sounding, the armed guards and the razor wire, he'd never make it out of the complex. Find a telephone? No. Vole had probably been telling the truth when she'd said they were blocked. And anyway, how could he get in touch with Alan Blunt or Mrs Jones at this late stage? They'd already be at the Science Museum.

Just one hour left.

Outside, over the din of the alarm, Alex heard another sound. The splutter and roar of a propeller. He went over to the nearest window and looked out. Sure enough, the cargo plane that had been there when he arrived was preparing to take off.

Alex was soaking wet, battered and almost exhausted. But he knew what he had to do.

He spun round and began to run.

ELEVEN O'CLOCK

Alex burst out of the house and stopped in the open air, taking stock of his surroundings. He was aware of alarms ringing, guards running towards him and two cars, still some distance away, tearing up the main drive, heading for the house. He just hoped that although it was obvious something was wrong, nobody would yet know what it was. They shouldn't be looking for him – at least, not yet. That might give him the edge.

It looked like he was already too late. Sayle's private helicopter had gone. Only the cargo plane was left. If Alex was going to reach the Science Museum in London in the fifty-nine minutes left to him, he had to be on it. But the cargo plane was already in motion, rolling slowly away from its chocks. In a minute or two it would go through the pre-flight tests. Then it would take off.

Alex looked around and saw an open-top army Jeep parked on the drive near the front door. There was a guard standing next to it, a cigarette dropping out of his hand, looking around to see what was happening – but looking the wrong way. Perfect. Alex sprinted across the gravel. He had brought a weapon from the house. One of Sayle's harpoon guns had floated past him just as he'd left the room and he'd snatched it up, determined to have something he could use to defend himself with at last. It would have been easy enough to shoot the guard right then. A harpoon in the back and the Jeep would be his. But Alex knew he couldn't do it. Whatever Alan Blunt and MI6 wanted to turn him into, he wasn't ready to shoot in cold blood. Not for his country. Not even to save his own life.

The guard looked up as Alex approached, and fumbled for the pistol he was wearing in a holster at his belt. He never made it. Alex used the handle of the harpoon gun, swinging it round and up to hit him, hard, under the chin. The guard crumpled, the pistol falling out of his hand. Alex grabbed it and leapt into the Jeep, grateful to see the keys were in the ignition. He turned them and heard the engine start up. He knew how to drive. That was something else Ian Rider had made sure he'd learned, as soon as his legs were long enough to reach the pedals. The other cars were closing in on him. They must have seen him attack the guard. The plane had wheeled round and was already taxiing up to the start of the runway.

He wasn't going to reach it in time.

Maybe it was the danger closing in from all sides that had sharpened his senses. Maybe it was his close escape from so many dangers before. But Alex didn't even have to think. He knew what to do as if he had done it a dozen times before. And maybe his training had been more effective than he'd thought.

He reached into his pocket and took out the yo-yo that Smithers had given him. There was a metal stud on the belt he was wearing and he slammed the yo-yo against it, feeling it click into place, as it had been designed to. Then, as quickly as he could, he tied the end of the nylon cord round the bolt of the harpoon. Finally, he tucked the pistol he had taken from the guard into the back of his combats. He was ready.

The plane had completed its pre-flight tests. It was facing down the runway. Its propellers were at full speed.

Alex slammed the gears into first, released the handbrake and gunned the Jeep forward, shooting over the drive and on to the grass, heading for the airstrip. At the same time there was a chatter of machine-gun fire. He yanked down on the steering-wheel and twisted away as his wing mirror exploded and a spray of bullets slammed into the windscreen and door. The two cars, speeding towards him, head-on, were getting closer and closer. Each of them had a guard in the back seat, leaning out of the window, firing at him. Alex swerved between them, and for a horrible second there was actually one on each side. He was sandwiched between the two cars, with guards firing at him left and right. But then he was through. The guards missed him and hit each other. He heard one of them yell out and drop his gun. One of the cars lost control and crashed into the front of the house, metalwork crumpling against brick. The other screeched to a halt, reversed, then came after him again.

The plane had begun to move down the runway. Slowly at first, but rapidly picking up speed. Alex hit the tarmac and followed.

His foot was pressed down, the accelerator against the floor. The Jeep was doing about seventy – not fast enough. For just a few seconds Alex was parallel with the cargo plane, only a couple of metres from it. But already it was pulling ahead. At any moment it would be in the air.

And straight ahead of him, the way was blocked. Two more Jeeps had arrived on the runway. More guards with machine-guns balanced themselves, half-crouching, on the seats. Alex realized the only reason they weren't firing was that they were afraid of hitting the plane. But the plane had already left the ground. Ahead of him, and just to his left, Alex saw the front wheel separate itself from the runway. He glanced in his mirror. The car that had chased him from the house was right on his tail. He had nowhere left to go.

One car behind him. Two Jeeps ahead of him. The plane now in the air, the back wheels lifting off. Everything happening at once.

Alex let go of the steering-wheel, grabbed the harpoon gun and fired. The harpoon flashed through the air. The yo-yo attached to Alex's belt spun, trailing out thirty metres of specially designed advanced nylon. The pointed head of the harpoon buried itself in the underbelly of the plane. Alex felt himself almost being torn in half as he was yanked out of the Jeep on the end of the cord. In seconds he was forty, fifty metres above the runway, dangling underneath the plane. His Jeep swerved, out of control. The other two Jeeps tried to avoid it – and failed. Both of them hit it in a three-way head-on collision. There was an explosion – a ball of flame and a fist of grey smoke that followed Alex up as if trying to snatch him back. A moment later there was another explosion. The second car had tried to avoid the two Jeeps but it had been travelling too fast. It ploughed into the burning wrecks, flipped over and continued, screeching on its back along the runway before it too burst into flames.

Alex saw little of this. He was suspended from the plane by a single thin white cord, twisting round and round as he was carried ever further into the air. The wind was rushing past him, battering into his face and deafening him. He couldn't even hear the propellers, just above his head. The belt was cutting into his waist. He could hardly breathe. Desperately he scrabbled for the yo-yo and found the control he wanted. A single button ... he pressed it. The tiny, powerful motor inside the yo-yo began to turn. The yo-yo rotated on his belt, pulling in the cord. Very slowly, a centimetre at a time, Alex was drawn up towards the plane.

He had aimed the harpoon carefully. There was a door at the back of the plane and when he turned off the engine mechanism in the yo-yo, he was close enough to reach out for its handle. He wondered who was flying the plane and where he was going. The pilot must have seen the destruction down on the runway but he couldn't have heard the harpoon. He couldn't know he'd picked up an extra passenger.

Opening the door was harder than he'd expected. He was still dangling under the plane and every time he got close to the handle the wind drove him back. He could still hardly see. The wind was tearing into his eyes. Twice his fingers found the metal handle, only to be pulled away before he could turn it. The third time, he managed to get a better grip but it still took all his strength to yank the handle down.

The door swung open and he clambered into the hold. He took one last look back. The runway was already three hundred metres below. There were two fires raging, but at this distance they seemed no more than match-heads. Alex unplugged the yo-yo, freeing himself. Then he reached into the waistband of his combats and took out the gun.

The plane was empty apart from a couple of

bundles that Alex vaguely recognized. There was a single pilot at the controls, and something on his instrumentation must have told him the door was open, because he suddenly twisted round. Alex found himself face to face with Mr Grin.

"Warg?" the butler muttered.

Alex raised the gun. He doubted if he would have the courage to use it. But he wasn't going to let Mr Grin know that.

"All right, Mr Grin," he shouted above the noise of the propellers and the howl of the wind. "You may not be able to talk but you'd better listen. I want you to fly this plane to London. We're going to the Science Museum in South Kensington. It can't take us more than half an hour to get there. And if you think about trying to trick me, I'll put a bullet in you. Do you understand?"

Mr Grin said nothing.

Alex fired the gun. The bullet slammed into the floor just beside Mr Grin's foot. Mr Grin stared at Alex, then nodded slowly.

He reached out and pulled the joy-stick. The plane dipped and began to head east.

TWELVE O'CLOCK

London appeared.

Suddenly the clouds rolled back and the midday sun brought the whole city, shining, into view. There was Battersea Power Station, standing proud with its four great chimneys still intact, even though much of its roof had long ago been eaten away. Behind it, Battersea Park appeared as a square of dense green bushes and trees that were making a last stand, fighting back the urban spread. In the far distance, the Millennium Wheel perched like a fabulous silver coin, balancing effortlessly on its rim. And all around it, London crouched; gas towers and apartment blocks, endless rows of shops and houses, roads, railways and bridges stretching away on both sides, separated only by the bright silver crack in the landscape that was the River Thames.

Alex saw all this with a clenched stomach, looking out through the open door of the aircraft. He'd had fifty minutes to think about what he had to do. Fifty minutes while the plane droned over Cornwall and Devon, then Somerset and the Salisbury Plains before reaching the North Downs and flying on towards Windsor and London.

When he had got into the plane, Alex had intended to use its radio to call the police or anyone else who might be listening. But seeing Mr Grin at the controls had changed all that. He remembered how fast the man had been both outside his bedroom and throwing the knife when Alex was handcuffed to the chair. He knew he was safe enough in the cargo area, with Mr Grin strapped into the pilot's seat at the front of the plane. But he didn't dare get any closer. Even with the gun it would be too dangerous.

He had thought of forcing Mr Grin to land the plane at Heathrow. The radio had started squawking the moment they'd entered London airspace and had only stopped when Mr Grin turned it off. But that would never have worked. By the time they'd reached the airport, touched down and coasted to a halt, it would have been far too late.

And then, sitting hunched up in the cargo area, Alex had recognized the two bundles lying on the floor next to him. They had told him exactly what he had to do.

"Eeerg!" Mr Grin said. He twisted round in his seat and for the last time Alex saw the hideous smile that the circus knife had torn through his cheeks.

"Thanks for the ride," Alex said, and jumped out of the open door.

The bundles were parachutes. Alex had checked them out and strapped one on to his back when they were still over Reading. He was glad that he'd spent a day on parachute training with the SAS, although this flight had been even worse than the one he'd endured over the Welsh valleys. This time there was no static line. There was no one to reassure him that his parachute was properly packed. If he could have thought of any other way to reach the Science Museum in the seven minutes he had left, he would have taken it. There was no other way. He knew that. So he had jumped.

Once he was over the threshold, it wasn't so bad. There was a moment of dizzying confusion as the wind hit him once again. He closed his eyes and forced himself to count to three. Pull too early and the parachute might snag on the plane's tail. Even so, his hand was clenched and he had barely muttered the word "three" before he was pulling with all his strength. The parachute blossomed open above him and he was jerked back upwards, the harness cutting into his armpits and sides.

They had been flying at four thousand feet. When Alex opened his eyes, he was surprised by his sense of calm. He was dangling in the air underneath a comforting canopy of white silk. He felt as if he wasn't moving at all. Now that he had left the plane, the city seemed even more distant and unreal. It was just him, the sky and London. He was almost enjoying himself.

And then he heard the plane coming back.

It was already a couple of kilometres away, but even as he watched he saw it bank steeply to the right, making a sharp turn. The engines rose and then it levelled out – it was heading straight towards him. Mr Grin wasn't going to let him get away so easily. As the plane drew closer and closer he could almost see the man's never-ending smile behind the window of the cockpit. Mr Grin intended to steer the plane right into him, to cut him to shreds in mid-air.

But Alex had been expecting it.

He reached down and took out the Nintendo. This time there was no game cartridge in it: but while he had been on the plane he had taken out Bomber Boy and slid it across the floor. That was where it was now. Just behind Mr Grin's seat.

He pressed the START button three times.

Inside the plane, the cartridge exploded, releasing a cloud of acrid yellow smoke. The smoke billowed out through the hold, curling against the windows, trailing out of the open door. Mr Grin vanished, completely surrounded by smoke. The plane wobbled, then plunged down.

Alex watched the plane dive. He could imagine Mr Grin blinded, fighting for control. The plane began to twist, slowly at first, then faster and faster. The engines whined. Now it was heading straight for the ground, howling through the sky. Yellow smoke trailed in its wake. At the last minute, Mr Grin managed to bring the nose up again. But it was much too late. The plane smashed into what looked like a deserted piece of dockland near the river and disappeared in a ball of flame.

Alex looked at his watch. Three minutes to twelve. He was still a thousand feet in the air and unless he landed on the very doorstep of the Science Museum, he wasn't going to make it. Grabbing hold of the cords, using them to steer himself, he tried to work out the fastest way down.

Inside the East Hall of the Science Museum, Herod Sayle was coming to the end of his speech. The entire chamber had been transformed for the great moment when the Stormbreakers would be brought on-line.

The room was caught between old and new, between stone colonnades and stainless steel floors, between the very latest in high-tech and old curiosities from the Industrial Revolution.

A podium had been set up in the centre for Sayle, the Prime Minister, the Press Secretary and the Minister of State for Education. In front of it were twelve rows of chairs – for journalists, teachers, invited friends. Alan Blunt was in the front row, as emotionless as ever. Mrs Jones, dressed in black with a large brooch on her lapel, was next to him. On either side of the hall, television towers had been constructed, with cameras focusing in as Sayle spoke. The speech was being broadcast live to schools throughout the country and it would also be shown on the evening news. The hall was packed with another two or three hundred people standing on first and second-floor galleries, looking down on the podium from all sides. As Sayle spoke, tape recorders turned and cameras flashed. Never before had a private individual made so generous a gift to the nation. This was an event. History in the making.

"...it is the Prime Minister, and the Prime Minister alone, who is responsible for what is about to happen," Sayle was saying. "And I hope that tonight, when he reflects on what has happened today throughout this country, he will remember our days together at school, and everything he did at that time. I think tonight the country will know him for the man he is. One thing is sure. This is a day you will never forget."

He bowed. There was a scatter of applause. The Prime Minister glanced at his Press Secretary, puzzled. The Press Secretary shrugged with barely concealed rudeness. The Prime Minister took his place in front of the microphone.

"I'm not quite sure how to respond to that," he joked, and all the journalists laughed. The Government had such a large majority that they knew it was in their best interests to laugh at the Prime Minister's jokes. "I'm glad Mr Sayle has such happy memories of our school-days together and I'm glad that the two of us, together, today, can make such a vital difference to our schools."

Herod Sayle pointed at a table slightly to one side of the podium. On the table was a Storm-breaker computer and next to it, a mouse. "This is the master control," he said. "Click on the mouse and all the computers will come on-line."

"Right." The Prime Minister lifted his finger and adjusted his position so that the cameras could get his best profile. Somewhere outside the museum, a clock began to strike.

Alex heard the clock from about three hundred feet, with the roof of the Science Museum rushing towards him.

He had seen the building just after the plane had crashed. It hadn't been easy finding it, with the city spread out like a three-dimensional map right underneath him. On the other hand, he had lived his whole life in west London and had visited the museum often enough. First he had seen the Victorian jelly mould that was the Albert Hall. Directly south of that was a tall white tower surmounted by a green dome: Imperial College. As Alex dropped, he seemed to be moving faster. The whole city had become a fantastic jigsaw puzzle and he knew he only had seconds to piece it together. A wide, extravagant building with church-like towers and windows. That had to be the Natural History Museum. The Natural History Museum was on Cromwell Road. How did you get from there to the Science Museum? Of course, turn left at the lights up Exhibition Road.

And there it was. Alex pulled at the parachute, guiding himself towards it. How small it looked compared to the other landmarks, a rectangular building with a flat grey roof, jutting in from the main road. Part of the roof consisted of a series of arches, the sort of thing you might see on a railway station or perhaps on an enormous conservatory. They were a dull orange in colour, curving one after the other. It looked as if they were made of glass. Alex could land on the flat part. Then all he would have to do was look through the curved windows. He still had the gun he had taken from the guard. He could use it to warn the Prime Minister. If he had to, he could use it to shoot Herod Sayle.

Somehow he managed to manoeuvre himself over the museum. But it was only as he fell the last two hundred feet, as he heard the clock strike twelve, that he realized two things. He was falling much too fast. And he had missed the flat roof.

In fact the Science Museum has two roofs. The original is Georgian and made of wired glass. But sometime in the recent past it must have leaked, because the curators have constructed a second roof of plastic sheeting over the top. This was the orange roof that Alex had seen.

He crashed into it feet-first. The roof shattered. He continued straight through, into an inner chamber, just missing a network of steel girders and maintenance ladders. He barely had time to register what looked like a brown carpet, stretched out over the curving surface below. Then he hit it and tore through that too. It was no more than a thin cover, designed to keep the light and dust off the glass underneath. With a yell, Alex smashed through the glass. At last his parachute caught on a beam. He jerked to a halt, swinging in mid-air inside the East Hall.

This was what he saw.

Far below him, all around him, three hundred people had stopped and were staring up at him in shock. There were more people sitting on chairs directly underneath him and some of them had been hit. There was blood and broken glass. A bridge made of green glass slats stretched across the hall. There was a futuristic information desk and in front of it, at the very centre of everything, was a makeshift stage. He saw the Stormbreaker first. Then, with a sense of disbelief, he recognized the Prime Minister standing, slack-jawed, next to Herod Sayle.

Alex hung in the air, dangling at the end of the parachute. As the last pieces of glass fell and disintegrated on the terracotta floor, movement and sound returned to the East Hall in an ever-widening wave.

The security men were the first to react. Anonymous and invisible when they needed to be, they were suddenly everywhere, appearing from behind colonnades, from underneath the television towers, running across the green bridge, guns in hands that had been empty a second before. Alex had also drawn his gun, pulling it out from the waistband of his combats. Maybe he could explain why he was here before Sayle or the Prime Minister activated the Stormbreakers. But he doubted it. Shoot first and ask questions later was a line from a bad film. But even bad films are sometimes right.

He emptied the gun.

The bullets echoed around the room, surprisingly loud. Now people were screaming, the journalists punching and pushing as they fought for cover. The first bullet went nowhere. The second hit the Prime Minister in the hand, his finger less than a centimetre away from the mouse. The third hit the mouse, blowing it into fragments. The fourth hit an electrical connection, smashing the plug and short-circuiting it. Sayle had dived forward, determined to click on the mouse himself. The fifth and sixth bullets hit him.

As soon as Alex had fired the last bullet, he dropped the gun, letting it clatter to the floor below, and held up the palms of his hands. He felt ridiculous, hanging there from the roof, his arms outstretched. But there were already a dozen guns pointing at him and he had to show them he was no longer armed, that they didn't need to shoot. Even so, he braced himself, waiting for the security men to open fire. He could almost imagine the hail of bullets tearing into him. As far as they were concerned, he was some sort of crazy terrorist who had just parachuted into the Science Museum and taken six shots at the Prime Minister. It was their job to kill him. It was what they'd been trained for.

But the bullets never came. All the security men were equipped with radio headsets and, in the front row, Mrs Jones had control. The moment she had recognized Alex she had spoken urgently into her brooch. *Don't shoot! Repeat – don't shoot! Await my command!*

On the podium, a plume of grey smoke rose out

of the back of the broken, useless Stormbreaker. Two security men had rushed to the Prime Minister, who was clutching his wrist, blood dripping from his hand. Journalists had begun to shout questions. Photographers' cameras were flashing and the television cameras, too, had been swung round to focus in on the figure swaying high above. More security men were moving to seal off the exits, following orders from Mrs Jones, while Alan Blunt looked on, for once in his life out of his depth.

But there was no sign of Herod Sayle. The head of Sayle Enterprises had been shot twice – but somehow he had disappeared.

YASSEN

"**Y**ou slightly spoiled things by shooting the Prime Minister," Alan Blunt said. "But all in all you're to be congratulated, Alex. You not only lived up to our expectations. You far exceeded them."

It was late afternoon the following day, and Alex was sitting in Blunt's office at the Royal & General building on Liverpool Street wondering just why, after everything he had done for them, the head of MI6 had to sound quite so much like a second-rate public school headmaster giving him a good report. Mrs Jones was sitting next to him. Alex had refused her offer of a peppermint, although he was beginning to realize it was all the reward he was going to get.

She spoke now for the first time since he had

come into the room. "You might like to know about the clearing-up operation."

"Sure..."

She glanced at Blunt, who nodded.

"First of all, don't expect to read the truth about any of this in the newspapers," she began. "We put a D-notice on it, which means nobody is allowed to report what happened. Of course, the ceremony at the Science Museum was being televized live, but fortunately we were able to cut transmission before the cameras could focus on you. In fact, nobody knows that it was a fourteen-year-old boy who caused all the chaos."

"And we plan to keep it that way," Blunt muttered.

"Why?" Alex didn't like the sound of that.

Mrs Jones dismissed the question. "The newspapers had to print something, of course," she went on. "The story we've put out is that Sayle was attacked by a hitherto unknown terrorist organization and that he's gone into hiding."

"Where is Sayle?" Alex asked.

"We don't know. But we'll find him. There's nowhere on earth he can hide from us."

"OK." Alex sounded doubtful.

"As for the Stormbreakers, we've already announced that there's a dangerous product fault and that anyone turning them on could get electrocuted. It's embarrassing for the Government, of course, but they've all been recalled and we're bringing them in now. Fortunately, Sayle was so fanatical that he programmed them so that the smallpox virus could only be released by the Prime Minister at the Science Museum. You managed to destroy the trigger, so even the few schools that have tried to start up their computers haven't been affected."

"It was very close," Blunt said. "We've analyzed a couple of samples. It's lethal. Worse even than the stuff Iraq was brewing up in the Gulf War."

"Do you know who supplied it?" Alex asked.

Blunt coughed. "No."

"The submarine I saw was Chinese."

"That doesn't necessarily mean anything." It was obvious that Blunt didn't want to talk about it. "You can just be sure that we'll make all the necessary enquiries—"

"What about Yassen Gregorovich?" Alex asked.

Mrs Jones took over. "We've closed down the plant at Port Tallon," she said. "We already have most of the personnel under arrest. Unfortunately we weren't able to talk to either Nadia Vole or the man you knew as Mr Grin."

"He never talked much anyway," Alex said.

"It was lucky that his plane crashed into a building site," Mrs Jones went on. "Nobody else was killed. As for Yassen, I imagine he'll disappear. From what you've told us, it's clear that he wasn't actually working for Sayle. He was working for the people who were sponsoring Sayle ... and I doubt they'll be very pleased with him. Yassen is probably on the other side of the world already. But one day, perhaps, we'll find him. We'll never stop looking."

There was a long silence. It seemed that the two spymasters had said all they wanted. But there was one question that nobody had tackled.

"What happens to me?" Alex asked.

"You go back to school," Blunt replied.

Mrs Jones took out an envelope and handed it to Alex.

"A cheque?" he asked.

"It's a letter from a doctor, explaining that you've been away for three weeks with flu. Very bad flu. And if anyone asks, he's a real doctor. You shouldn't have any trouble."

"You'll continue to live in your uncle's house," Blunt said. "That housekeeper of yours, Jack Whatever, she'll look after you. And that way we'll know where you are if we need you again."

Need you again. The words chilled Alex more

than anything that had happened to him in the past three weeks. "You've got to be kidding," he said.

"No." Blunt gazed at him quite coolly. "It's not my habit to make jokes."

"You've done very well, Alex," Mrs Jones said, trying to sound more conciliatory. "The Prime Minister himself asked us to pass on his thanks to you. And the fact of the matter is that it could be wonderfully useful to have someone as young as you—"

"As talented as you—" Blunt cut in.

"—available to us from time to time." She held up a hand to ward off any argument. "Let's not talk about it now," she said. "But if ever another situation arises, perhaps we can get in touch then."

"Yeah. Sure." Alex looked from one to the other. These weren't people who were going to take no for an answer. In their own way, they were both as charming as Mr Grin. "Can I go?" he asked.

"Of course you can," Mrs Jones said. "Would you like someone to drive you home?"

"No thanks." Alex got up. "I'll find my own way."

*   *   *

He should have been feeling better. As he took the lift down to the ground floor, he reflected that he'd saved thousands of schoolchildren, he'd beaten Herod Sayle and he hadn't been killed or even badly hurt. So what was there to be unhappy about? The answer was simple. Blunt had forced him into this. In the end, the big difference between him and James Bond wasn't a question of age. It was a question of loyalty. In the old days, spies had done what they'd done because they loved their country, because they believed in what they were doing. But he'd never been given a choice. Nowadays, spies weren't employed. They were used.

He came out of the building, meaning to walk up to the tube station, but just then a cab drove along and he flagged it down. He was too tired for public transport. He glanced at the driver, huddled over the wheel in a horribly knitted, home-made cardigan, and slumped on to the back seat.

"Cheyne Walk, Chelsea," Alex said.

The driver turned round. He was holding a gun. His face was paler than it had been the last time Alex saw it and the pain of two bullet wounds was drawn all over it, but – impossibly – it was Herod Sayle.

"If you move, you *bliddy* child, I will shoot you," Sayle said. His voice was pure venom. "If you try anything, I will shoot you. Sit still. You're coming with me."

The doors clicked shut, locking automatically. Herod Sayle turned round and drove off, down Liverpool Street, heading for the City.

Alex didn't know what to do. He was certain that Sayle planned to shoot him anyway. Why else would he have taken the huge chance of driving up to the very door of MI6 headquarters in London? He thought about trying the window, perhaps trying to get the attention of another car at a traffic light. But it wouldn't work. Sayle would turn round and kill him. The man had nothing left to lose.

They drove for ten minutes. It was a Saturday and the City was closed. The traffic was light. Then Sayle pulled up in front of a modern, glass-fronted skyscraper with an abstract sculpture – two oversized bronze walnuts on a slab of concrete – outside the front door.

"You will get out of the car with me," Sayle commanded. "You and I will walk into the building. If you think about running, remember that this gun is pointing at your spine."

Sayle got out of the car first. His eyes never

left Alex. Alex guessed that the two bullets must have hit him in the left arm and shoulder. His left hand was hanging limp. But the gun was in his right hand. It was perfectly steady, aimed at Alex's lower back.

"In..."

The building had swing-doors and they were open. Alex found himself in a marble-clad hall with leather sofas and a curving reception desk. There was nobody here either. Sayle gestured with the gun and Alex walked over to a bank of lifts. One of them was waiting. They got in.

"The twenty-ninth floor," Sayle said.

Alex pressed the button. "Are we going up for the view?" he asked.

Sayle nodded. "You make all the *bliddy* jokes you want," he said. "But I'm going to have the last laugh."

They stood in silence. Alex could feel the pressure in his ears as the lift rose higher and higher. Sayle was staring at him, his damaged arm tucked into his side, supporting himself against the door. Alex thought about attacking him. If he could just get the element of surprise. But no... They were too close. And Sayle was coiled up like a spring.

The lift slowed down and the doors opened.

Sayle waved with the gun. "Turn left. You'll come to a door. Open it."

Alex did as he was told. The door was marked HELIPAD. A flight of concrete steps led up. Alex glanced at Sayle. Sayle nodded. "Up."

They climbed the steps and reached another door with a push-bar. Alex pressed it and went through. He was back outside, thirty floors up, on a flat roof with a radio mast and a tall metal fence running round the perimeter. He and Sayle were standing on the edge of a huge cross, painted in red. Looking around, Alex could see right across the city to Canary Wharf. It had seemed a quiet spring day when Alex left the Royal & General offices. But up here the wind streaked past and the clouds boiled.

"You ruined everything!" Sayle howled. "How did you do it? How did you trick me? I'd have beaten you if you'd been a man! But they had to send a boy! A *bliddy* schoolboy! Well, it isn't over yet! I'm leaving England. Do you see...?"

Sayle nodded and Alex turned to see that there was a helicopter hovering in the air behind him. Where had it come from? It was red and yellow, a light, single-engine aircraft with a figure in dark glasses and helmet hunched over the controls. The helicopter was a Colibri EC120B, one of the quietest in the world. It swung round over him, its blades beating at the air.

"That's my ticket out of here!" Sayle continued. "They'll never find me! And one day I'll be back. Next time, nothing will go wrong. And you won't be here to stop me. This is the end for you! This is where you die!"

There was nothing Alex could do. Sayle raised the gun and took aim, his eyes wide, the pupils blacker than they had ever been, mere pinpricks in the bulging whites.

There were two small, explosive cracks.

Alex looked down, expecting to see blood. There was nothing. He couldn't feel anything. Then Sayle staggered and fell on to his back. There were two gaping holes in his chest.

The helicopter landed at the centre of the cross. Yassen Gregorovich got out.

Still holding the gun that had killed Herod Sayle, he walked over and examined the body, prodding it with his shoe. Satisfied, he nodded to himself, tucking the gun away. He had switched off the engine of the helicopter and behind him the blades slowed down and stopped. Alex stepped forward. Yassen seemed to notice him for the first time.

"You're Yassen Gregorovich," Alex said.

The Russian nodded. It was impossible to tell what was going on in his head. His clear blue eyes gave nothing away.

"Why did you kill him?" Alex asked.

"Those were my instructions." There was no trace of an accent in his voice. He spoke softly, reasonably. "He had become an embarrassment. It was better this way."

"Not better for him."

Yassen shrugged.

"What about me?" Alex asked.

The Russian ran his eyes over Alex, as if weighing him up. "I have no instructions concerning you," he said.

"You're not going to shoot me too?"

"Do I have any need to?"

There was a pause. The two of them gazed at each other over the corpse of Herod Sayle.

"You killed Ian Rider," Alex said. "He was my uncle."

Yassen shrugged. "I kill a lot of people."

"One day I'll kill you."

"A lot of people have tried." Yassen smiled. "Believe me," he said, "it would be better if we didn't meet again. Go back to school. Go back to your life. And the next time they ask you, say no. Killing is for grown-ups and you're still a child."

He turned his back on Alex and climbed into the helicopter cabin. The blades started up and a few seconds later the helicopter rose back into the air. For a moment it hovered at the side of the building. Behind the glass, Yassen raised his hand. A gesture of friendship? A salute? Alex raised his hand. The helicopter spun away.

Alex stood where he was, watching it, until it had disappeared in the dying light.

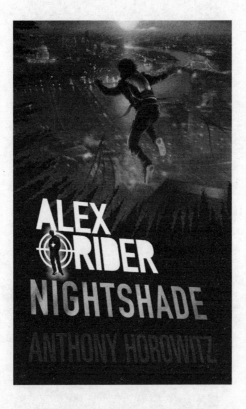

**NIGHTSHADE IS COMING.
AND ALEX IS ALONE.**

Turn over for an exclusive sneak
peek of the first chapter...

EXCLUSIVE EXTRACT FROM NIGHTSHADE

The British Airways Airbus A318 had been kept in a holding pattern before it landed at Heathrow. Looking out of the window, Alex Rider watched the familiar landmarks slide beneath him for a third time. There was the River Thames, snaking its way past Slough and Maidenhead. Then Windsor Castle, built in the eleventh century and now home to the Queen, visible for miles around. In the distance, he could see the first high-rise apartments springing up around the edge of London.

He glanced at Jack Starbright who was dozing in the seat next to him. The two of them were on their way back from a long weekend in Amsterdam ... a treat they had promised themselves ever since they had returned from Smoke City, the industrial compound in Wales where Alex had come face-to-face with the Grimaldi brothers, the last two survivors of the criminal organization known as Scorpia. The Grimaldis had been planning the kidnap of the century, code name Steel Claw, and would have succeeded if Alex hadn't stumbled across their path. But it had been a close thing. Alex still woke at night remembering the huge steam train that had come blasting through the night, chasing him as he made for the single tunnel that provided the only means of escape.

So much had happened in the past few weeks. He had thought Jack was dead but discovered she was still alive. That in itself had changed everything for him, lifting a huge weight off his shoulders and giving him a fresh start. She had once been his housekeeper but she had become his closest friend and he had been unable to manage without her. At the same time, he had left America, picking up the pieces of his old life in London: his home, his friends. Jack had gone back to her studies – she hoped to become a lawyer – while Alex had gone back to school. As an added bonus, the two of them had suddenly found themselves with more money than they had ever known. They would be secure for life.

They had earned a weekend away together. It had been an opportunity to walk along the canals, to visit art galleries and coffee shops, to do some shopping, to relax and enjoy life. Above all, they had spent time together, laughing off everything that had happened in the last few weeks. Even Mrs Jones, the head of MI6 Special Operations, had urged him to leave his adventures behind him and settle down to a more ordinary life. Alex was convinced that his time as a spy was all behind him now.

He was wrong.

The aircraft had just passed over Cookham, an attractive village on the banks of the River Thames and if Alex had been able to look down twenty thousand feet, he would have watched for himself as a murder – which had been planned to the last detail several weeks before – was finally put into action.

The security officer sitting outside Clifford Hall on the edge of Cookham had noticed the plane circling and knew at once that it was flight BA 423 from Amsterdam. But then he knew the flight path of every plane that took off from or landed at Heathrow, just as he knew the names of everyone who lived in the village. He could even recognize them by their car number plates: the plumber in his white van, the local magistrate in her Volvo, the bank manager in his new Ford Fiesta. He was sitting in a folding chair next to the main gates with a newspaper in his lap. But he had not read a word of it. His job was to watch, to be ready, always to stay alert. And although he looked half-asleep, his hand was never very far away from the Glock 17 semi-automatic pistol which fitted snugly into the thumb release paddle holster clipped on to his belt, under his jacket. If necessary, he could load, take aim and fire with total accuracy in less than two seconds.

His name was Robert Spencer. He had been Second Lieutenant in Afghanistan until a roadside bomb had crippled him, ending his military career. He was now a senior officer in Protection Command, a highly specialized division of the London Metropolitan Police. His job was to look after the man who lived at Clifford Hall.

James Clifford – now Lord Clifford – had been a politician for more than forty years, but perhaps the most remarkable thing about him was that in all that time he had always been popular. He was a man who loved his country, who worked hard, who wanted to make a difference. He had been an extremely effective Home Secretary – in fact he had been so successful in his war on organized crime that, when he retired, it was decided that he should be given round-the-clock protection ... just in case. He had, after all, made plenty of enemies.

He was retired now and lived with his wife in the handsome country villa that his family had owned for generations. Clifford Hall had the look of a French château, with five bedrooms, a conservatory and a perfect lawn that led all the way to the river with a view of Lock Island on the other side of a narrow stretch of water. Second Lieutenant Spencer had been given a flat above the garage. There were CCTV cameras everywhere and, sitting in front of a bank of screens in his front room, he could see anyone who came near. Life in an English village is very much a matter of routine and after all the time he had spent in Cookham, he had most of the day pinned down to the minute. 8.10am – the newspapers delivered. 8.25am – the mail. 9.00am – Mrs Winters, the cleaning lady, arrives. 10.15am – Lady Clifford walks the dogs. And so on. There was almost no chance that anyone would seriously try to hurt Lord Clifford but, as Spencer knew from his time in the army, "almost" wasn't good enough. He took his job seriously. And he liked Lord Clifford. He wanted to keep the old man safe.

As the British Airways flight curved out of sight, he became aware of two figures approaching the gate and the short, curving drive that led to the front door. His hand slid a few centimetres towards his gun, then stopped as he saw that the visitors were young girls, no more than twelve years old, dressed in the blue and red polo shirts that identified them as Girl Guides. One of them was carrying a wooden tray with a pile of chocolate muffins. They stopped in front of him.

"How can I help you girls?" Spencer asked.

"Hello. My name is Amy and we're raising money for our local activity centre," the first of them replied. She had fair hair, framing a very attractive face, blue eyes and a scattering of freckles over her cheeks.

"We made them ourselves," the other said. She was a year or two younger, a black girl with glasses and hair tied back in pigtails. "I'm Jasmine," she added.

"They're fifty pence each."

"Or you can buy three for a pound."

Spencer smiled. "That's very kind of you, but I'm afraid I'm not into cakes." He patted his stomach. "I have to watch my weight."

"Would the people in the house like to buy some?" Jasmine, the girl with the pigtails, asked.

"I don't think so." Spencer shook his head. The truth was that he wouldn't allow anyone to pass through the gates unless they were expected; not even someone as innocent as a Girl Guide.

But then a voice called out behind him. "I'd love a chocolate muffin. I'll have it with my afternoon cup of tea."

Spencer turned round. The front door was open. As luck would have it, Lord Clifford had chosen that moment to come into the garden for a little fresh air. Spencer stood up as the man he was paid to protect, arrived at the front gate. He was wearing a blue blazer and a straw hat to shield himself from the hot sun and he was supporting himself on a walking stick. He had suffered a heart attack earlier that summer and he still hadn't fully recovered his health. But he showed no sign of that as he stopped at the gate and smiled at the two new arrivals. "Do you live in Cookham?" he asked.

"No, sir. We live in Taplow."

Taplow was another village, further down the river.

"And you made these yourselves?"

"Yes, sir."

"I can bring a couple of muffins up for you if you like, sir," Spencer said.

"No, no. That's all right, Robert." The old man fumbled in his pocket for loose change. "What did you two young ladies say you were collecting for?"

"It's for our activity centre," Amy repeated.

"We need to repaint our hut," Jasmine explained.

"And we're buying new equipment for the kitchen."

"Well, that's a very good cause." Lord Clifford drew out a shiny pound coin. "I only want one of your cakes, but you can keep the change."

"Thank you!" the girls chorused.

One of them held up the tray. "You can help yourself to whichever one you want."

Lord Clifford licked his lips, then reached out and took the biggest muffin from the top of the pile. "It smells delicious!" he exclaimed.

He took a bite.

Fifteen minutes later, the plane touched down and taxied towards Terminal 5 before coming to a halt. Alex and Jack unbuckled their seat belts and reached up for their luggage, which included the great ball of Dutch cheese that Jack had insisted on buying in an Amsterdam market. Alex stuffed his exercise books into his backpack. He had school the next day and had been doing his homework during the flight.

At the same time, Lord Clifford suffered the first seizure that would lead to a major heart attack, followed by death.

Nobody guessed that he had been murdered and that the muffin he had eaten had been made with flour, eggs, milk, butter, chocolate and sodium cyanide, a lethal poison that had begun to attack his heart and lungs the moment he had taken the first bite. Twenty-four hours later, the two Girl Guides had left the country. Protection Command made no further enquiries and so they did not realize that there was no activity centre in Taplow, no hut to repaint, no kitchen needing equipment.

The organization known as Nightshade had killed Lord Clifford for one simple reason. His death would give them the opportunity to launch a major terrorist attack on the city that was Alex's home. The attack would take place in exactly three weeks' time.

READ OTHER GREAT BOOKS BY
ANTHONY HOROWITZ...

Alex Rider – you're never too young to die…

Alex Rider has 90 minutes to save the world.

High in the Alps, death waits for Alex Rider…

Once stung, twice as deadly. Alex Rider wants revenge.

Sharks. Assassins. Nuclear bombs. Alex Rider's in deep water.

He's back – and this time there are no limits.

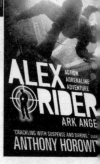

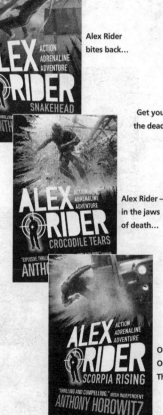
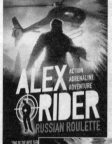

COLLECT ALL OF THE HILARIOUS

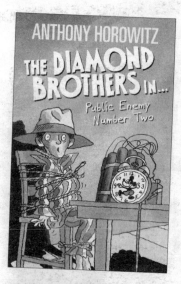

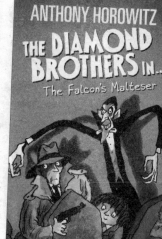

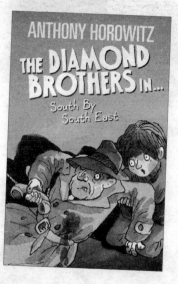

"Horowitz is the perfect writer. His dialogue crackles with hardboiled wit."

Frank Cottrell Boyce, *Guardian*

DIAMOND BROTHERS INVESTIGATIONS

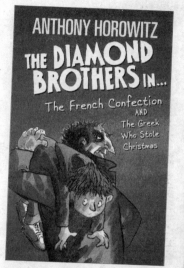

Tim Diamond is the world's worst private detective, and unfortunately for his quick-thinking brother, Nick, the cases keep coming in. What connects them? Murder! And if the Diamond Brothers don't play their cards right, they could be next!

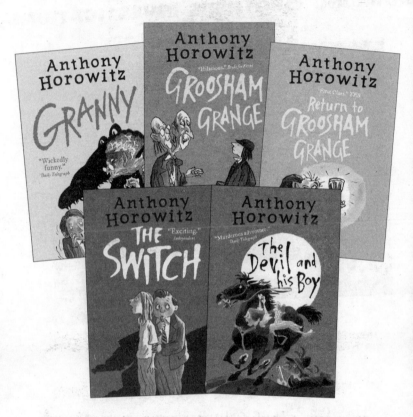

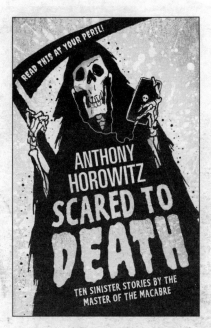

SOMETIMES
YOUR NIGHTMARES BECOME REAL...

This terrifically twisted and wickedly funny collection of spine-tingling short stories is only recommended for the most fearless of readers.

"A deliciously macabre collection of horror stories told with lashings of gruesome relish."
THE BOOKSELLER

Anthony Horowitz is the author of the number one bestselling Alex Rider books and the Power of Five series. He enjoys huge international acclaim as a writer for both children and adults. After the success of his first James Bond novel, *Trigger Mortis*, he was invited back by the Ian Fleming Estate to write a second, *Forever and a Day*. His latest crime novel, *The Sentence is Death*, featuring Detective Daniel Hawthorne, was a bestseller. Anthony has won numerous awards, including the Bookseller Association/Nielsen Author of the Year Award, the Children's Book of the Year Award at the British Book Awards, and the Red House Children's Book Award. He has also created and written many major television series, including *Collision*, *New Blood* and the BAFTA-winning *Foyle's War*. He lives in London with his wife, two sons and his dog, Boss.

You can find out more about Anthony and his work at:
www.alexrider.com
@AnthonyHorowitz